VIRGIL'S AENEID
Retold for
Young Adults

FRANK HERING

CONTENTS

ACKNOWLEDGMENTS

I would like to thank Susan Howe, the Latin teacher at Elgin Academy, for giving me the idea for this project and for her feedback on what should be included in it. And I would like to thank my wife, Beth, and my son, Zachary, for their love and support.

A NOTE TO READERS

Over two thousand years ago, the Roman poet Virgil wrote the epic chronicling the Trojan hero Aeneas' quest to establish a new homeland, the city that will one day become Rome. While stories about the dictates of fate and about gods helping their children may seem old-fashioned, the story still speaks to the issues of our times, issues of war and peace, love and loss, duty and pleasure, privilege and self-determination, the triumph of battles won and the tragedy of battles lost, new countries founded on lands occupied by others and immigrants excluded by established residents.

Virgil's Aeneid Retold for Young Adults retells the myth in modern English. Preserving the order and major events and characters of the original, this book makes the *Aeneid* accessible to readers unfamiliar with the grand poetic style and length of ancient epic. Having taught high-school students since 2000, I hope this book will inspire students to read the *Aeneid* itself, either in translation or in Latin. There are many translations of the work, and new ones appear each year. I would recommend the translation by Stanley Lombardo from Hackett (2005),

1

which also contains an excellent introduction by W.R. Johnson. Lombardo strikes a balance between modern English poetically rendered and the lofty language of epic poetry, between a swift-moving narrative and a contemplative voice aware of complexity. I enjoy reading many translations of a text, so after Lombardo, readers may want to search out others. Robert Fitzgerald's 1983 translation remains one of my favorites, though it is more challenging to read, so I would not start with it. And of course, there are the Homeric texts, the *Iliad* and the *Odyssey*, which strongly influenced Virgil. Translations by Lombardo, Robert Fagles, and Fitzgerald are excellent.

I have included an extensive glossary describing major characters and providing the pronunciation of their names, which students preparing to read Virgil's poem in their English or Latin classes will find very useful. Finally, I have provided discussion questions to help readers begin to think about themes, characterization, and literary technique. A number of the questions ask readers to think about the situations and motivations of minor characters, such as Iarbas and Amata, and the leadership qualities of Dido. One of the most important themes in the book is *pietas*, a sense of duty to the gods, one's country, and one's parents and ancestors (probably in that order). *Pietas* was a central virtue for the Romans. Virgil often gives Aeneas the epithet *pius*, which I translate as devout or pious.

PROLOGUE

The Judgment of Paris

All of the gods had been invited to the wedding of the devout Peleus and the sea goddess Thetis. All, that is, except Eris, the goddess of discord. The insult infuriated her, so she rolled a golden apple, inscribed "To the Fairest," into the wedding feast. Three goddesses claimed it: Venus, the goddess of passion; Minerva, the goddess of battle wisdom; and Juno, the queen of the gods. They asked Jove to decide which of them was the fairest, but he knew better; whichever one he chose, the other two goddesses would be angry at him. So, Jove told them that Paris, a prince of Troy, had shown himself to be a very impartial judge. He would decide.

So, each goddess displayed herself before Paris and offered him a bribe. Minerva assured him of great success in war. Juno would make him the king of both Europe and Asia. Venus promised him the most beautiful woman in the world, Helen, the daughter of Jove and Leda. Paris awarded the golden apple to Venus and eagerly awaited his prize.

But Helen was the wife of Menelaus, King of Sparta. This was not an obstacle for Venus. The goddess of passion easily brought about a burning, torrid love affair that resulted in Paris bringing Helen to Troy as his wife. Furious, Menelaus sought the help of his powerful brother, Agamemnon, King of Mycenae, and together they gathered the Greek forces and brought more than a thousand ships to Trojan shores. Minerva and Juno, goddesses insulted, looked forward to seeing the Trojans wiped from the face of the earth.

BOOK ONE

Aeneas and the Queen of Carthage

The rage of Juno, Queen of the Gods, stormed after the ships carrying Aeneas and his Trojan refugees. Her undying heart still seethed with anger, even after the destruction of Troy. All because Paris, a Trojan prince, had chosen Venus as more worthy of the golden apple than she. How dare he disrespect Juno, who walked the halls of Olympus in majesty as the wife of Jove, King of the Gods? Now another prince of Troy, Aeneas, was preventing her from wiping out the Trojans once and for all.

But there was something more. She knew the Fates had decreed that Aeneas would establish a homeland in Italy. He would father descendants that would eventually create Rome, whose might would destroy Carthage, the land she loved most. The arrogant conquerors of her beloved city would come from Trojan stock!

Because of her rage, she called upon Aeolus, keeper of the winds, to release the gusts that would capsize the Trojan ships.

5

Unbridled winds now charged across the sea and kicked up waves that towered over the refugees. Storm clouds brought on darkness broken only by the lightning. As thunder cracked, Aeneas watched as wave after wave sacked his fleet.

Beneath the surface, Neptune, God of the Sea, felt the deep waters around him churn. Raising his seaweed-covered head above the surface, he spotted Aeneas' ships in danger. Already men bobbed in the water surrounded by the treasures they had saved from the looting of Troy. Knowing this was his sister Juno's handiwork, he shook his head in disgust as seawater streamed down his hair and beard. Neptune was ready to seek revenge on the winds and their keeper. They must pay dearly for disturbing the sea that was his alone to command. But, on second thought, he decided it would be better now to calm the troubled waters. There would be time later to seek payback. He used his trident to divert the stampede of winds and to tame the waves.

As Aeneas' sailors collapsed on the deck, panting, he looked out over the sea and saw how much of his fleet had been lost. Heaving a sigh, he thanked the gods for sparing a few ships to continue their quest for a new home. He scanned the horizon and saw land. Knowing his men were desperate to feel solid ground under their feet, he directed his ships to the African coast of Libya.

Once ashore, Father Aeneas fought through his exhaustion to hunt meat for his hungry men while his companion-in-arms, Achates, built a fire. After his men had eaten, Aeneas rallied them with winged words. "Trojans, we are not strangers to hardship. Someday, it will help to recall even these torments. Perhaps doing so will bolster our determination to endure a future misfortune. For now, remember the gods have promised us a glorious homeland in Italy. The Fates have decreed this. My mother, Venus, assures me of this." Thus, pious Aeneas, known for his devotion to the gods, his country, and his parents, stifled his anguish and feigned confidence for the sake of his fated duty.

✳✳✳

Ruling from high heaven, Jove, King of the Gods, looked down upon the earth. He gazed in delight at the calm seas reflecting images of his beloved clouds. He scanned the outspread lands and checked on the nations of man. His great eyes paused at the sight of Carthage when he saw his daughter Venus, the shining Goddess of Love, rise from the seafoam at its coast.

She glided through the clouds and approached her father, eyes glistening with tears. "Father, what grudge do you hold against my son Aeneas, the hero most devoted to the gods? Did you forget all the long-horned cattle he sacrificed to you? Why do you keep him from Italy?"

Smiling, Jove replied, "Daughter, my wife Juno sends the man hardship after hardship. You know how she wants to wipe out the Trojans and keep Rome from sacking her beloved Carthage. But she will relent. She'll have to. Let me show you a jet stream of my thoughts, the one that will bring about Aeneas' glorious fate. See? Your son will wage a great war against the barbarous tribes of Italy. He will build the city walls of Lavinium and rule over his people for three years. His son Ascanius, also called Iulus, will rule for thirty years and establish another kingdom, one called Alba Longa. There, his descendants will rule for three centuries. Then Ilia, royal priestess of Vesta, will give birth to twins by Mars, the God of War. One of them, Romulus, will go on to build the Walls of Mars and name his people the Romans, after himself. As you can see, for them, the current has no end. The Fates and I, as always, are of one mind on this."

***

As Dawn spread through the morning sky, Aeneas took his trusted companion Achates with him to scout the strange land. Soon, they came across a huntress, looking for all the world like the goddess Diana.

"Hail, strange sirs," she cried to them. "Have you seen my sister? She outran me when we were chasing a boar. She is dressed like me. Tyrian women often wear knee-length tunics, carry quivers, and cover their feet with high purple boots."

"I have not seen your sister," Aeneas replied, "but surely you are one of the immortals; your radiant face gives it away. Perhaps you are Apollo's sister, Mistress of the Hunt and the Bow, like the one you carry there. I pray to you, goddess, tell me where we are."

"I would never consider myself Diana's equal, strange sir. But I will tell you that this is Carthage, a new city Queen Dido is building on the Libyan shore. Our story is full of intrigue, but I'll relate it briefly.

"Dido's brother, Pygmalion, King of Tyre, cut down her husband, Sychaeus, whom she loved dearly. But her brother hated their marriage and was mad for her husband's gold. Sychaeus was the richest man in all Phoenicia, you know. Anyway, the King kept the death of his sister's husband a secret. Then one night, the ghost of Sychaeus came to her in a dream, bared his gory chest, and told how her brother, the King, had murdered him! He urged flight and showed her where he had buried his riches, untold amounts of gold and silver. Hah! She took her husband's hidden treasure, gathered those who hated the tyrant's rule, seized ships, and brought us here. When we arrived, this clever woman asked the Berber King Iarbas to sell her a piece of land, only as much as an ox-hide could encompass. He agreed. Then Dido cut the ox-hide into thin strips and laid them out around a hill. What a massive amount of land she got! Now she builds walls around the newfound city of Carthage! But who are you, strange sirs, and where are your ships?"

"Maiden, we are refugees from Troy, the city sacked by the will of the gods. We wander the seas in search of a homeland, but a storm has driven us here. I am Aeneas, known for my devotion to the gods, and my fame reaches the sky. I am the son of Venus, and she directs our desire towards Italy. But the twenty ships I left Troy with are now only seven."

"The gods must have brought you here to Carthage. Just continue on this road to Queen Dido. I foretell you will find your men safe with her. But I must continue to search for my sister." With that, the maiden turned and walked away. As she did so, her gorgeous tresses tumbled down, and saffron robes now swept her ankles. Under each step, flowers sprung up and sent forth ambrosial perfume. Aeneas now knew; he had received a visit from his mother.

Venus' aid did not end there. She cloaked Aeneas and his companion Achates in a mist so that no one could see the strangers and challenge them with questions.

***

Wanting to survey the expanse before them, Aeneas and Achates climbed a high hill. They expected to find a group of huts. Instead, they were amazed. Already, Dido's people had built perimeter walls, which surrounded a forum and paved roads. Busy as bees in a flowering springtime field, these refugees from Tyre were building houses and even a theater. Before Aeneas' very eyes, they were establishing laws, choosing officials, and gathering a senate.

"Blessed are they who see their city walls rising high," Aeneas exclaimed.

Achates looked at his captain and replied, "Son of the goddess, one day soon, we too will begin the foundations for an even greater homeland!"

The two men now walked through the city gates, unchallenged even in their Trojan armor. Venus's cloaking mist continued to make them invisible.

In the middle of the city, the Carthaginians had built a temple dedicated to Juno. Aeneas and his companion mounted the steps to its bronze threshold and, walking abreast, entered through its doors. Aeneas stopped, stared in wonder, and began to weep. For on the temple's walls were scenes from the Trojan War, exhibited in sequence:

Paris brings to Troy the beautiful Helen, daughter of Jove and wife of Menelaus.

One thousand Greek ships amass on the shores of Troy and are met by Trojan spears.

Achilles, in his chariot, routs the forces of Troy and keeps them behind the walls built long ago by Neptune and Apollo.

His priest scorned, Apollo, God of the Silver Bow, shoots arrows of plague at the Greek camps, and funeral pyres burn night and day.

Now, the enraged Achilles sulks in his tents, refusing to fight for Agamemnon, the general who insulted him.

Glorious Hector leads his troops across the plains of Troy, as Jove sends them victory after victory.

Ulysses, wearing his boars-tusk helmet and accompanied by Diomedes, raids the camp of Rhesus, killing Thracian men in their sleep, and stealing the marvelous horses before they even have a taste of Trojan fodder.

And there, behind the walls of Troy, the doomed child Astyanax cries in the arms of Hector, afraid of his father's helmet with the horse-hair crest; his mother, Andromache, pleads with her husband to stay.

The burning Greek ships at his back, Patroclus, disguised as Achilles, leads his troops and drives the Trojans back to their walls.

Now Hector kills the great Patroclus, thus summoning the wrath of Achilles, who fills the Scamander River with bloody Trojan corpses.

And glorious Hector is slain by Achilles, who drags the corpse behind his chariot three times around the walls of Troy.

Priam kisses the man-killing hands of Achilles and offers gold to ransom a dearly loved son's desecrated body.

Trojan allies join the war: Memnon, son of Dawn, with his Ethiopians; Queen Penthesilea and her Amazons, women warriors who destroy even the best men.

Apollo flies Paris' arrow into swift-footed Achilles; Telamon Ajax defends the corpse with his massive shield.

Then Aeneas saw himself battling the best of the Achaeans as they spill from the belly of a horse rising high above him.

Turning in the center of the room, Aeneas followed the course of the murals. When his eyes completed the circuit, he saw Dido entering the temple, surrounded by many of her people. Aeneas gazed in admiration as the refugee queen assigned work and motivated her retinue to build their kingdom. The Queen took her throne, and then—marvel of marvels—Aeneas' missing captains approached Dido in supplication.

"Dear Queen," the oldest of them began, "we are Trojans and represent those few who have survived the sack of our city. We have traveled seven years in search of the homeland the gods have granted us in Italy. Storms at sea have nearly destroyed us, and we have lost our great Father, the hero Aeneas, known for his piety. We beg you to allow us to repair our ships and gather supplies so we can go in search of our goddess-born leader."

"Rise. My own tragedies and hardships make me sympathize with you Trojan refugees. As you can see from our murals, we know of mighty Troy's fall. I will send my best shipwrights to help you with your repairs, and I will provision your ships so you can continue your journey. Or you can join us as equals in building this new city. Furthermore, I will send out search parties in the hope of finding Aeneas. We too long to see him."

At that moment, Venus dissolved the mist surrounding her son and his companion. Dido and all those around her drew back in surprise at seeing these two men suddenly appear. The goddess had lavished her grace on Aeneas, made him taller, more massive in size so that he would appear godlike before this queen.

"Hail, Dido! I am Aeneas, known for my devotion to the gods, and my fame reaches the sky. I am the son of Venus, and she directs our desire towards Italy. Thank you for accepting us as your suppliants and may the gods grant you your heart's desire: a mighty kingdom that your descendants will rule for generations to come!"

With that, Aeneas embraced his dear comrades.

***

Deeply moved by the Trojans' reunion, Dido rose from her throne and spoke. "Come, let us sacrifice to the gods so they may have their due and we may have a feast." She led them all to her palace and sent servants to get sacrificial animals for both the queen's guests and the Trojans still gathered on the Libyan shore. Aeneas sent Achates for Ascanius and for gifts, treasures rescued from the sack of Troy.

Taking the form of a serving maid, Venus surveyed the feast and brooded on the sanctuary her son had found in the land of Juno. Then, quick as a thought, she entered the room of her son Cupid and said to him, "Your brother is not safe yet. You, my arsenal, must take the form of Ascanius and present the Trojan gifts to Dido, who is sure to fawn over you. Then, you must inflame her heart with a passion for Aeneas so that she will do all she can to help him. Meanwhile, I will cause my beloved grandson to fall asleep and carry him to Cythera, the island devoted to me."

With that, Cupid dashed down to Aeneas' ship and, staring at the face of the sleeping Ascanius, assumed the boy's features. The moment Venus left with her grandson cherished in her arms, Achates arrived, carrying gifts for the Queen, and led the little sneak to the palace.

Meanwhile, Dido poured a libation to the gods and then passed around the bejeweled goblet to her guests. Aeneas, duped, welcomed Ascanius and told his pride and joy to present the Queen with these gifts: a robe embroidered in gold and an ambrosial veil that Helen herself wore. Adoring these treasures from Troy, Dido was even more taken with Aeneas' son (or rather, with the god's deceptive presence). Cupid now stared into the Queen's eyes and saw a widow's devotion to her husband's memory. He teased this out and shot into her mind a young woman's desperate desire for the hero Aeneas.

No longer interested in the boy, Dido turned to her goddess-born guest and implored him to tell of Troy's fall and the seven years he had wandered since then.

BOOK TWO

The Fall of Troy

Although my mind shudders at the thought of remembering such unspeakable horrors, I will begin. For ten long years, we awoke every morning to the same sight: a thousand ships at our shoreline and Greek camps all along our beach. But when the sun rose for the last time on the splendor of Troy, we couldn't believe our eyes. A turquoise sea winged with whitecaps instead of sails and an empty landscape whose only feature was a giant wooden horse that rose as high as the city walls.

Troy now streamed through the Scaean Gates. Giddy from long confinement behind the god-built walls, we rushed down to the plain to explore the Greek camp.

"Here is where Achilles sulked in his tent."

"This must be where they had Patroclus' funeral pyre."

But most stood around the great horse.

"What is it?"

"Did they leave it as a gift for us?"

"Maybe it was going to be a siege machine."

Now the arguments began.

"We should haul it inside our gates and dedicate it to Neptune, God of the Horse."

"Into the sea with it!"

"No, set it ablaze and turn it into a huge bonfire, to celebrate our triumph over the Greeks."

Suddenly, shepherds dragged a young man—a Greek—before our king. He wore only a white loincloth, and around his head were sacred ribbons. He looked terrified. Upon Priam's command, the shepherds released the man, and he immediately fell to his knees. "King of kings, I beg you to spare my life. Don't judge me by my looks! The Greeks are no friends of mine. I can be useful to you. I can tell you how to save Troy from Ulysses' tricks!"

Suppliants are sacred to the gods, so we listened to his story.

"I was to be a human sacrifice, but I escaped and hid in the marshes until these men found me. Here, let me tell you about Ulysses' treachery. Perhaps you have heard the name of Palamedes, King of Euboea. I was his closest companion-in-arms, and while he lived, I had respect and riches. But the liar Ulysses hated the man and falsely accused him of treason, trumped-up charges. After they executed Palamedes, I was crazy with grief, and fool that I was, I shot my mouth off, saying that one day I would avenge my king.

"Well, Ulysses started to plot against me. He cornered our great seer, Calchas. He's the one who told us that the only way we could sail to Troy was by first sacrificing Agamemnon's virgin daughter to Diana. Now, Ulysses forced Calchas to lie. One day, the great seer went into a trance and exclaimed, 'With the blood of a virgin slain you came to Troy, only with the blood of the Greek slain will you return home.' Calchas would not say who 'the Greek' was. Ulysses commanded him to speak, but the seer wouldn't. Then Ulysses beat him, but they had prearranged this. So, the seer, at last, said my name ... But what's the use. You don't believe me. I can see you glancing at each other. You'll let your people stone me. Ulysses will love that!"

We saw the terror in his eyes; we saw his trembling. So we begged him to continue.

"Well, all too soon, the terrible day arrived; I was washed and then dressed for the blood sacrifice. At the last minute—I admit it— I ran away and hid in the marshes. The Greeks must have found another to sacrifice; they're not here anymore. But please, I renounce Greece; accept me into your country, and I will serve the Trojan army well."

He again fell to the ground and assumed the ritual position of the suppliant. Priam, as kindly as a father welcoming home a penitent son, raised him and commanded us to accept him as one of us. We did. We were such fools. Then, we asked him about the giant horse.

And now, dear Queen, you will hear Ulysses' masterpiece and see why he is known as the man of many twists and turns.

✳✳✳

Sinon, with apparent gratitude, continued, "By the gods' sacred ribbons that I now wear, I swear I will tell the truth to my new countrymen. Here's another of the liar Ulysses' many tricks. As you know, he and Diomedes snuck into your citadel and stole that great protector of Troy, the Palladium. Maybe they thought it wouldn't be a sacrilege if they, Pallas' favorite heroes, were the ones to steal it. Fools! They killed the guards and then handled the effigy of Minerva with their bloody hands! No sooner did they get the image into our camp than the omens started. The statue's eyes kindled with fire; sweat poured down its limbs. And, I know you won't believe this, but I swear it is true, the image of the goddess herself flashed out of the statue and, in her rage, raised her shield and pointed her spear at us!

"The seer Calchas announced that we had to leave Troy and return only after appeasing the wrath of Minerva and gaining more of the gods as allies. The wooden horse is an offering to the goddess, to make up for the Palladium.

"But Ulysses turned even this into a trap. Calchas said that if you were to take the offering into your city, Troy would sack Agamemnon's Mycenae. So, Ulysses told the builder to make the horse so large that you wouldn't be able to get it through the wall's gates. He hoped you'd think it a siege machine and burn it or roll it into the sea. Then Minerva's wrath would turn on Priam, and Troy would be no more."

Most of us believed Sinon, but everything he said from the moment we laid eyes on him was a lie created by Ulysses.

Then Laocoon, a priest of Neptune, ran down from the citadel, armed and furious. "My people, have you gone mad? Do you think the Greeks simply gave up and went home? Does that sound like the cunning Ulysses you know? Search the belly of this hollow horse, and you will find it pregnant with their soldiers, waiting to get inside our impenetrable walls and slit our throats. Oh, my people, beware of Greeks and their gifts."

Then, with all his might, he threw his spear into the pine ribs of the horse. It stuck there, and the echo reverberated for all to hear. Just as we started to consider the priest's warning, someone screamed and pointed towards the water. Two giant sea serpents swam to our shore. We ran, but each snake snatched up one of Laocoon's sons, coiled around the young body, and began to feed. The priest tried to fight them, to pull apart the spirals that were strangling his sons. But his hands could gain no purchase on the serpents' slimy skin. Then they joined forces and pulled the priest in opposite directions. Leaving Laocoon torn in two, the sea serpents slithered away and coiled themselves around Minerva's temple.

We were terrified. What would happen next? Many prayed to the goddess. Others murmured that Laocoon got what he deserved for desecrating Minerva's offering. Finally, Priam announced, "We must, with all due reverence, bring the horse inside the city walls." One group began to widen the entrance. Another group put rollers under the monstrosity. Finally, all of us pushed and pulled it towards the city. The gods had so clouded our minds that we ignored the sounds of weapons clanging around inside the cavernous horse. We ignored the screams of Cassandra, princess and seer, standing outside the Scaean Gates. Staring in horror at Priam's splendid city, she cried, "Troy is in flames, the city walls are bathed in blood, a monstrous birth pours from the horse's womb!" But fools that we were, we ignored her visions.

That night, after sacrificing to the gods and feasting on skewered meat, we celebrated our great success. The Greeks were gone! The wooden horse and Athena's protection were now ours! We would repay the Greeks' visit with one of our own and lay siege to Agamemnon's city! Then exhausted from dragging our own destruction into the city and celebrating like idiots, we stumbled off to our beds.

When the drunk sentries passed out, Sinon signaled the Greek fleet hidden on the other side of Tenedos, an island nearby. He then released the belly of the beast and birthed the hidden soldiers into the dark night. They got the jump on us and killed many sleeping Trojans. Sinon unlocked the gates, and Greece streamed into Troy.

And so the lies and tricks of Ulysses did what ten years of war and a thousand ships could not, what godlike Achilles and the mighty Telamon Ajax failed to do: defeated the might and splendor of Troy.

***

That night, Hector appeared in my dreams. He was standing at the foot of my bed, his hair and beard matted with blood, his whole body covered in gore and dirt, his feet pierced by Achilles so he could drag our hero around Troy. How different he was from how I remembered him: Hector striding into Troy wearing Achilles' gleaming armor after killing Patroclus, Hector throwing torches to set fire to the Greeks' ships.

Tears streaming down his dust-covered cheeks, Hector called out, "Goddess-born Aeneas, why are you sleeping? You must flee the city. Troy is on fire, and the enemy holds the city walls. The time for fighting has passed. If someone could have saved Priam's city, I would have done so. Carry the city's sacred objects, our public penates, with you. Let them share in your fate as you wander to establish a new city." And with that, he held out Vesta's statue and the sacred flame.

I jolted awake, smelled the smoke, and heard the cries, even though my father Anchises' house was set back and screened by trees. I climbed to the roof and looked out over a city engulfed in flames and confusion. Now, too late, I understood the Greeks' deception. Recklessly, I put on my armor, grabbed my weapons, ready to answer the call of the blaring trumpets.

I gathered what soldiers I could, including young Coroebus, who had come to our city mad to marry Cassandra and give Priam a son-in-law to fight for Troy. But even he failed to believe his intended bride's warning. My men assembled, I shouted to them, "Remember the only hope for the conquered is to fight without hope."

How can I describe the horrors of that night? Where there weren't flames, there was blood. We followed a line of Trojan dead into the heart of the city.

But Agamemnon's men paid the price for this night as well. We came upon a party of Greek soldiers, who mistook us for friends. Their captain hailed us, "Did you just come from your ship? You're missing all the fun and plunder!" But by the time he realized his error, we had already cut down him and his men.

This gave Coroebus an idea. "Son of the goddess, let's put on their armor and see if we can trick other Greeks. Two can play at their game." We quickly swapped our bloody armor for theirs.

Suddenly, we heard Coroebus howl, a look of horror on his face. Then we saw. In the distance, the lesser Ajax, the son of Oileus, was dragging Cassandra by her hair from the temple of Minerva, wrists bound tight, gown torn. The sight made Coroebus furious, and he plunged, sword drawn, into Greek troops. They killed him immediately. We were ready to avenge his death and save Cassandra, but then spears hit us from above. The gods did not make Trojans for deception. Unlike the Greeks, we were caught in our own trap. Trojan soldiers on the roof mistook us for the enemy.

Now we saw the king's palace overwhelmed. We rushed toward it, knowing we would die, but determined to go down fighting. And I swear by those dead who were near and dear to me that had my fate allowed it, I would have died gloriously in battle too.

Priam's household, staring death in the face, pried treasures from the walls to launch as missiles against the onslaught of Greek troops, who continued to swarm. Hearing a familiar battle cry, we turned our heads and saw Achilles—no, his son, Pyrrhus, shining in his father's god-made armor. He and his men slashed through the guards stationed in front. Now, swinging a great battle-ax over his head, Pyrrhus cut down the thick bronze doors. Through them, we could see Priam, terrified. Seeing the enemy in his doorway, the old king put on his armor, long unused, and took up his useless sword.

His wife, Hecuba, huddled with her daughters behind a courtyard altar, now broke cover. "Husband, have you lost your mind?" she wailed. "Troy is gone; even my Hector, were he still with us, could not hold them off. Come to the altar. Either it will protect you or you'll die with us." Then, letting his sword clatter to the ground, he allowed his wife to lead him to his daughters.

Polites, one of Priam's sons, now ran through the courtyard, pursued by swift-footed Pyrrhus. Polites reached the altar and looked at his mother and father. But suddenly, a spear point burst forth from his chest, splattering his parents with their own child's blood. Behind Polites stood the gruesome Pyrrhus.

The old king pulled himself up from the consecrated ground on which he had been seated and, shaking with old age and fury, wailed, "You ... you monster. How can you kill my son before my very eyes? Achilles showed me mercy and respect, but you ..." Unable to say more, Priam threw his feeble spear, which only bounced off Pyrrhus' bronze shield.

"Then go to my father and tell on me. Tell him what a bad boy I've been." With that, Pyrrhus grabbed the great king and dragged him by the hair to an altar, Priam's feet slipping in his son's blood. Then Achilles' son buried his sword up to the hilt in the old man's side.

And now, Priam, once the mightiest king in Asia, lies on the shore, a headless corpse without a name.

✱✱✱

From a distance, Priam reminded me of my own dear father, Anchises. He and the King were of the same age. They had been young men together the last time Troy had been sacked, by Hercules and his companion-in-arms Telamon. My mind had been so set on revenge that I had forgotten what I should never have forgotten: my vulnerable father, my darling son, and my lovely wife. My troops were nowhere to be seen, so I turned to run home. Nothing should have stopped me, but then I saw Helen, cowering behind another one of the courtyard altars. Fury rose in me when I saw her. Her wild affair with Paris had brought destruction to Troy.

But now, my mother appeared to me in her divine form. She had never done so before. "My dear son, what terrible grief causes this rage of yours? Have you forgotten your father, Anchises, now weak with old age? Greek soldiers surround his house. He, along with Ascanius and Creusa, would now be dead if not for my protective care. Shining Helen is not to blame for the fall of Troy. The gods themselves are responsible. Don't give me that look. It is true. Here, let me remove the mist of mortality from your eyes. You will see something terrible, something no mortal should ever see, but I think you require this."

With new eyes, I surveyed the scene around me. My gods! Before, I had seen the impenetrable city wall crumbling. Now, I saw an enraged Neptune, using his great trident to pry up the walls that he himself had built. Before, I had seen Greek troops going berserk through the streets of Troy. But now, I saw the mighty Juno, wearing her battle armor, waving on Agamemnon's army with her divine sword. Most horrifying of all, I looked up and saw the battle goddess, Minerva, standing on the roofs of Trojan palaces, shaking the aegis, awful to behold, its gorgon head making a terrible, roaring sound.

I turned to my mother, and she said, "Now, you see the gods themselves are destroying Troy. Head home. I will lead you safely through the streets."

When I reached Anchises' house, I put down my sword and shield and prepared to carry my father. But he refused. "I am too old to go somewhere else. I survived one sacking of Troy; another is too much to ask. You go. You are young and strong."

We all pleaded with him to no avail. So I picked up my sword and shield again and said, "Did you think I could abandon you to frenzy and flames, to leave unburied a body that had slept beside a goddess?"

Then, a miracle. A holy flame danced above our Ascanius' head, licking but not burning his locks and temples. My wife and I strove to douse the fire, but Anchises looked up to the heavens and cried, "Olympian Jove, is this a sign, a reward for our piety?" Suddenly, thunder boomed on our left and a comet streaked across the night sky. My father bowed his head and said, "Pious Aeneas, I will go with you now. The father of gods and men has great plans for our family."

I put my dear father on my back and had one of the household slaves give my father the public penates, for my hands were bloody from combat. I told the rest of the household where to meet us, took my son's hand, and told my wife to stay close behind me.

Earlier, I went boldly through the streets, but now with my family around me, I moved very cautiously. Suddenly my father exclaimed, "Run, Aeneas! I can see their gleaming armor from here!" For the first time that night, I panicked. As I ran, Anchises' arms tightened around my neck, and I squeezed Ascanius' wrist tighter as he struggled to keep up. Finally, we reached the spot where the others had already gathered. With a sigh of relief, I let go of my son's hand and let my father down gently. I turned to smile and hug my wife … but she was not there, and no one had seen her. She must have fallen behind during our flight.

For the second time that night, I panicked, running back through the streets, calling out her name, not caring if the enemy heard me. Reaching Anchises' house, now overwhelmed by flames and Greeks, I started to go inside, when the ghost of my wife blocked me. Three times, I tried to embrace her, and three times, she slipped through my arms.

Finally, she said, "Dear Aeneas, what terrible grief causes you such frenzy? You cannot take your Creusa with you. Jove will not allow it. You must endure many travels, but at last, you will arrive at Hesperia. There, a royal wife and kingship will be yours. Do not grieve for me. Take care of our son." Then, she faded away.

I rejoined our party; many more had joined us. I consoled my dear Ascanius, picked up my father, and led my people into the mountains.

BOOK THREE

Other Trojans and a New Troy

We spent the winter gathering the supplies we would need to search for a new homeland. When we took to the sea, the first place we landed was Thrace. A land dear to Mars, Thrace had been an ally of Troy. We decided to build our new city there.

One day, in preparing to sacrifice to the gods, I visited a small mound of earth, upon which grew several small trees. As I started to pull up one of the saplings, I saw blood pooling on the ground. An inauspicious sign, but I tried pulling out another one. There, too, blood emerged, and now I heard a groan coming from under the ground. "Aeneas," it said. "Why are to rending my flesh? Stop desecrating my corpse. I am your countryman, Polydorus, Priam's son. My father sent me and a great treasure to Thrace, asking its king to keep us both safe until the war's end. Wanting to keep the gold for himself, he had his men kill me. They threw their spears, which pinned me to the ground. I was left unburied, but eventually, the ground covered me, and the spears' wood began to set down roots and send forth branches. Leave me be, and flee this traitorous land!"

Terrified, I consulted my father, who said we must bury Polydorus so his spirit could go to the Underworld. After giving him all due honors, we launched the ships once more.

Unsure of where to go, we decided to seek a message from the Oracle at Delos, the island of Apollo's birth. It offered sanctuary to my weary people, while I prayed in the god's ancient temple. "Apollo, God of Prophecy, tell us, what is the will of Jove? Where should we establish a new Troy, one that will endure?"

The ground shook, and my hair stood on end. Then, a loud voice. "Goddess-born, the Trojans must seek their ancient mother. In that land, the sons of Aeneas shall rule for generations without end."

"The god must mean Crete," my father, Anchises, argued, "the land from which Teucer came."

But when we arrived there, the city penates, the ones I had rescued from sacked Troy, visited me in a dream. "Apollo repeats the message he gave you on Delos. Your sons will rule an empire without end. You must seek out your ancient mother—not Teucer's Crete, but a country the Greeks call Hesperia and the natives call Italy. This is the land from which Dardanus came."

Sharing this awe-inspiring visitation with my father, he recalled that Troy had dual ancestors and ordered us again to launch our ships.

Driven off-course by storms, we first landed at the Strophades. Finding plenty of cattle grazing there, we prepared a sacrifice for the gods and a feast for ourselves. But before we could bite into the skewered beef, down from the skies came the Harpies, horrible creatures with the faces of women and the bodies of birds. They attacked us with their talons and dropped their foul excrement on our food.

We prepared another feast, but this time, I had most of my men lie in ambush. When the Harpies swooped down, we attacked them, but to no avail. One of the monstrous birds perched herself on the prow of one of our ships and spoke. "Goddess-born Aeneas, leave our island. You are not welcome here. I am Celaeno, leader of the Harpies, and the gods have given me prophetic powers. Yes, you will reach Italy, but you will not raise your city walls until hunger drives you to eat your own tables." She then led her monstrous followers into the forest.

✳✳✳

While traveling through Western Greece, we heard a bizarre rumor: Priam's son Helenus was ruling over lands in the kingdom of Achilles' son, the bloodthirsty Pyrrhus. I had to speak to him, to learn about this new homeland he ruled. Sailing off the eastern coast of Corcyra, we sighted Epirus and walked inland to the city of Buthrotum.

Shocked beyond belief, we came upon Hector's widow, Andromache. She was pouring libations next to a replica of the Simois River, made to look like the one in Troy. The widow was calling Hector's spirit to a tomb she called his. Upon recognizing our Trojan arms, she fainted. In our Trojan armor, we had some difficulty convincing her we were real and not the ghosts of Hector and his men. But eventually, eyes downcast, she told us, "Pyrrhus, the man whose father killed my dear

Hector, took me as plunder and made me a slave to his bed. After we had two sons, he grew tired of me. Before he left to claim a new wife, he gave me to another one of his slaves, Priam's son Helenus. Pyrrhus married Hermione, the daughter of Menelaus and Helen. Then, thank the gods, he was killed by Agamemnon's son, Orestes, the man to whom she had first been promised. Helenus rules this land, this memory of Troy."

Down from the citadel came Helenus and his entourage. Weeping, he welcomed us and walked us to the walls of Little Troy. My Trojans were overjoyed, and I kissed the pretend Scaean Gate. In his great hall, we prepared a sacrifice to the gods and a feast for ourselves.

After a few days, I sought Helenus' counsel. I was worried, especially after what the harpy had told us. "Son of Priam, priest of Apollo, like your sister Cassandra, you are a powerful seer. Tell me what you can of our journey to Italy so I can prepare."

We went into the shrine of Apollo, and after performing the sacred rites, Helenus went into a trance and chanted, "Son of the Goddess, you must endure many trials before you reach your journey's end. But reach Italy, you shall. Jove, allied with the Fates, has decreed this. When you first sight Italy, avoid the coast of the sea we share. Head for Sicily, but take the long way around the island. For in the channel between Sicily and Italy lurk Scylla and Charybdis. The former is a monster whose six mouths snatch men from their ships. The latter is a whirlpool that sucks the sea down and spews it up again several times a day. Above all, worship Juno and give her many sacrifices to appease her anger.

"Leaving Sicily, you will come to the western coast of Italy. Seek Cumae, and visit the Sibyl there. She receives prophecies from Apollo and in her frenzy writes them on leaves, which she then stores in her cave. However, she must give you a prophecy from her own lips. She will help you reach your destination. No more will the gods allow me to tell you."

With tears in his eyes, Helenus led me to my ships, which his servants had loaded with gifts. Crying, Andromache approached Ascanius and said, "Take this Trojan cloak and these tunics, which I made myself. Wear them with pride, and show the world what my beloved Astyanax would have looked like. He too would be approaching the end of childhood."

We followed Helenus' directions carefully. After struggling to avoid Charybdis, we reached Sicily and spent a dreadful night there, as Mt. Etna erupted in the distance. In the morning, a man, who was nothing but skin and bones, came upon us and embraced me at the knees in ritual supplication. "Dear Trojans, I beg you. Take me away from this place. Yes, I am a Greek, but the horrors I have faced here have punished me for any wrong I did to Troy."

I told him to rise and explain what had happened. "I came to this land as one of Ulysses' men. His curiosity got us caught in the cave of the Cyclops Polyphemus. That gigantic monster ate several of our men, dashing out their brains and splattering the walls with their gore before eating them raw, bones and all. Ulysses, pretending he wanted to curry favor with Polyphemus, offered him strong wine unmixed with water. The Cyclops passed out drunk, belching up red wine and my comrades' limbs. Then, we stabbed him in his one great eye. But in the rush to the ships, I was left behind. Now, we must leave, no time to lose. There are a hundred Cyclopes like him on this island. I beseech you in the name of Jove, protector of suppliants, take me anywhere you are going, anywhere but here."

No sooner had he finished speaking than we saw Polyphemus walking blindly to the shore. As he washed out his empty eye socket, we snuck aboard our ships. But quiet as we were, he heard us and reached out, groping. When he couldn't find our boats, he stood up and roared, as loud as Mt. Etna. This brought many of his brothers down to the beach. Imagine the horror! All those one-eyed giants staring at us as we rowed for our lives. Thankfully, we were out of their reach by then.

After sailing around Sicily with our new companion, we eventually came to Drepanum. Here, I lost my dear father, Anchises, a loss that neither Celaeno nor Helenus had told me about. Only with great effort did I leave his grave behind and continue my mission. Some god then drove us to your welcome shores.

Thus, steadfast Aeneas finished the tale of his great wanderings.

BOOK FOUR

The Tragedy of Dido

Dido was enthralled. Hounded by suitors, she had easily rejected them all. She had stayed true to her widow's vow never to love another man. But Aeneas' tale had quickened her dormant passion. Lying in bed that night, she could not sleep, kept awake by the pounding of her heart and by feverish dreams that inflamed her body. She did not know about the wound from Cupid. Instead, she credited Aeneas' massive build, his divine origins, and his heroic actions in war.

Confessing all this to her sister, Dido anxiously awaited her advice. "For too long," Anna began, "you have buried your youth in your husband's grave. The spirits of the dead don't care about such devotion. It is one thing to reject suitors you have no desire for. It is another to deny yourself the pleasures of a man you yearn for so powerfully. And think of the kingdom he could help you create, the kingdom that the children you'd have with him would rule!"

For the next few days, Dido and Anna made sacrifices at each shrine, praying that the gods would look kindly on a union with Aeneas. Each afternoon, the Queen walked beside the object of her desire, showing him all of Carthage's allure. Each night, she held another feast for her guests and pleaded with Aeneas to tell his story again.

Meanwhile, her people sat idle. The theater was left half-finished, the army did not practice maneuvers, and the great walls no longer climbed towards the heavens.

Juno, seeing the Queen of her Carthage so lovesick, knew who to blame. Confronting Venus, she said, "Well, you and Cupid must be happy with yourselves, two gods defeating a mortal woman."

"I don't know what you're talking about," Venus replied.

"I know all about your fear of a mighty Carthage, afraid that it will challenge the supremacy of your son's future kingdom. But come now. There's no reason for us to work at cross purposes. We can rule these people together. Let Aeneas marry Dido. Carthage shall be her dowry."

Venus knew this was a trick; Juno would never allow her city to submit to another. Plus, she knew the Queen of the Gods had it in for Aeneas. So she proceeded with caution. "That's an offer I can't refuse. However, do you think the Fates mean for these two cities to be one? Do you think Jove will allow this? You know how he punishes gods who try to thwart his plans."

Haughtily, Juno replied, "Leave my husband to me. I'll take care of all that. You and I must make sure that the two lovers are married tomorrow. As the Goddess of Marriage, I will be there to consecrate their nuptials."

Venus nodded, but smiled to herself at Juno's duplicity.

Shortly after dawn, Carthaginian and Trojan nobles gathered for a day of hunting. Aeneas wore a cape of Tyrian purple, embroidered with gold thread, a gift made by Dido's own hands. She, in turn, wore the Trojan cloak Ascanius had presented to her at that first banquet. Each of the lovers looked like a god. Venus had made her son's chest and shoulders wider, and down from his brow, she ran curls as thick as clusters of hyacinth flowers. Likewise, Juno darkened Dido's black hair, put a warm glow in her brown eyes, and made her skin shine like the burnished-gold clasp that held her mantle together.

The beaters set off ahead of them, flushing Libyan game. The lovers, riding abreast, brought up the rear, the arrows clattering in their quivers. Then Juno floated dark clouds over the hunting party and rolled thunder across the open field. Torrents of rain scattered the hunters, each small group hurrying to find shelter.

Soaked but happy, the lovers found a cave, one they could have all to themselves. Their eyes met and held in a shared understanding. The Goddess of Marriage made her presence felt by allowing the lightning outside to create a gentle glow around them. With husky voices, they spoke of their commitment, each to the other, thus loosening the restraint on their desire. Woodland nymphs sang wildly in the distance. The lovers, though embracing in secret, nevertheless called this moment their wedding.

In the weeks that followed, Dido and Aeneas spent much of their time engaged in lovemaking. When he wasn't in Dido's bed, Aeneas was busy directing the workers in their building projects, the army in its maneuvers, and the senators in passing of laws. The Trojan refugees, though unsure whether this was their Fate, worked alongside the Carthaginians.

Meanwhile, rumors of the Queen's dalliance reached the ears of her suitors, and they were furious. King Iarbas, son of Jupiter Ammon and an African nymph, called upon his father to avenge this outrage. "Why sacrifice to almighty Jove when all you get are empty arms while some foreign pretty-boy gets the prize?"

On Olympus, Jove heard his son and directed his gaze to the shores of Libya. He saw that the fledgling city had made significant progress in recent weeks. Where there had been huts, Aeneas now stood with houses and towers rising around him. So Jove called upon Mercury to deliver a message to the lingering hero. Strapping on his golden, winged sandals and taking up the Caduceus, Mercury soared above the clouds until he came to North African Atlas, who planted his feet among the Berber tribes of King Iarbas and held up the sky. Here, Mercury hovered for a moment and then plunged to the Great Sea. He skimmed the water, like a tern that glides between the waves hunting for fish, the salt spray just barely wetting the tips of its wings. Landing on Libyan shores, Mercury strode toward Aeneas, who was directing the construction of a great port.

"So, Aeneas, are you building the foundations of your lady's city? I don't think Venus saved your life for that. Have you forgotten the kingdom awaiting you in Italy? What do you hope to gain by dallying with the Libyan Queen? If you have forgotten your own glory, at least think of Ascanius Iulus."

The god's presence filled Aeneas with a sense of awe, but the taunting annoyed him. Now, however, the messenger's tone and demeanor changed, and Aeneas felt the hairs on the back of his neck stand up.

"I bring you a message from almighty Jove, who is always allied with Fate. Leave Carthage! Deny pleasure and take to your ships!" With that, Mercury dashed off faster than the blink of an eye.

Aeneas was left pale and trembling. He wanted to flee immediately, even though he loved Carthage's Queen. Mercury's words had terrified him. But what would he say to Dido? He called his captains over, told them to gather the Trojans together, and begin to prepare the ships for launching. He would postpone telling the Queen until the time was right.

But before long, the rumor of Aeneas' preparations reached Dido. She ran through the city streets in a frenzy, as a Maenad raves through the mountains when called to Bacchus' wild rites. Such was Dido's rage. Finding Aeneas, she screamed in his face, "Traitor! Did you plan to sneak away after all of the promises we spoke to one another? Because of you, the surrounding chieftains hate me and threaten my new city. My own people laugh at me. Because of you, I violated the promise I made on my husband's tomb and gave up my only chance for undying glory."

With tears in his eyes and a husky voice, Aeneas replied, "Dear Dido, I wasn't going to steal away without giving you an explanation. And please know that I am incredibly grateful to you and will cherish the time we had together for as long as I live. If my destiny were my own, I would be content to stay beside you and help make Carthage a mighty city. But you know that Jove, who is always allied with the Fates, has decreed that I am to build a Trojan citadel in Italy, which Iulus and generations to come will rule after me."

Sobbing, Dido clasped Aeneas' knees and begged, "Please, Aeneas, please, if you have any love left for me, if you have ever felt kindly towards me, reconsider. Let Carthage be the land for your Trojans, the land that you and Ascanius rule over."

Aeneas' heart was breaking; he wanted to take Dido in his arms and agree to everything she asked. But when he thought of Jove's command, his limbs again began to tremble. So he spoke firmly to Dido, "I swear to you, Mercury just visited me in broad daylight and gave me Jove's stern message: 'Leave Carthage! Deny pleasure and take to your ships!' I cannot defy the gods, not even for you."

Still suffering from Cupid's wound, Dido was deaf to his reasoning. Madly she loved Aeneas. She screamed, "You are no son of Venus. You know nothing of love or passion. You have a heart of stone." She ran off, sobbing. Longing to go after her, to comfort her, Aeneas pushed down his rising pity, turned, and set off for his ships.

✳✳✳

Dido prayed for her death. She asked her worried sister, Anna, to have a pyre built so she could burn the clothes, armor, and weapons that Aeneas left in her room and use dark magic to break free from her thralldom. Secretly, she had other plans.

His preparations made, Aeneas tried to get some sleep by his ships before he launched them in the morning. But that night, Mercury reappeared, warning, "Child of the goddess, now is not the time for sleep. Dido has gone mad because she is losing you. She is capable of anything: burning your ships, sending her Tyrian navy in pursuit, killing herself. You must leave now! Not a moment to lose!" Aeneas roused his Trojans, ordered the men to take the oars, and himself cut the cables anchoring them to Libya.

When Dawn left Tithonus' loving arms to bring morning light to gods and men, Dido looked from her tower and saw an empty beach. The Trojans had sailed! She could see the white water created by their oars. "I could have killed them all and strewn the Carthaginian harbor with their limbs!" she cried out. "Now, they're gone, but I am not powerless. By Juno, the goddess who protects my city, and by Hecate, the dread goddess of sorcery who meets her suppliants at the crossroads, may there forever be war between Aeneas' people and mine! When Carthage achieves its destiny and controls the Mediterranean, let an avenger rise from my ashes."

Tears falling rapidly, Dido put a torch to the pyre and climbed to the top of it, plucking Aeneas' sword from the items she was going to burn. "Let cruel Aeneas see these flames and may the smoke carry to him my curse.

Her sister, Anna, arrived and saw the Queen thrust the sword deep into her heart. She screamed. "Was this your plan all along, Dido?" On the decks of their ships, Trojans pointed to the Libyan shore and wondered about the glowing flames and billowing smoke. Remembering Mercury's warning about what Dido might do, Aeneas was filled with a gloomy foreboding.

BOOK FIVE

A Homeland in Sicily

D riven by the winds back to Sicily, Aeneas' ships rested on the shores where Acestes lived. He was the son of a Trojan mother and a river god. Wearing a bearskin, Acestes welcomed the refugees from Troy.

Since they were near Anchises' tomb, Aeneas gave an offering to his father's spirit. Gathering his people together, he announced, "To commemorate the first anniversary of Anchises' death, we will compete in athletic games: a ship race, a foot race, an archery contest, and a boxing match. Prizes and glory to the winners!"

On Aeneas' command, Ascanius led to the grounds a troop of boys his own age, riding stallions and dressed in full armor. They paraded before their fathers, whose proud eyes filled with tears as they recognized traces of their ancestors' faces. The troop now split in two and advanced on each other in war games, performing their maneuvers, as intricate as the Labyrinth in Crete. When he became King of Alba Longa,

Ascanius would revive the equestrian display, and later, the Romans would celebrate this ancestral tradition, calling the boys on horseback "the Trojan Troop."

While the men competed, the women gathered near the shore. They wept for the dead Anchises. And they wept for themselves as they looked out over the endless expanse of sea. How weary they were, and how much sailing they still had to do! Juno, enraged by Aeneas' flight and Dido's death, stirred up trouble among these Trojan women. She sent Iris to whisper in their ears, "Seven long years at sea! Seven years homeless! Aeneas has already rejected the homes offered to us at Little Troy and Carthage. Let's fire the ships so that we will have to make a city of Trojans here, in the land of Acestes!" The women, inspired by the goddess, put firebrands to the wood and cloth.

Now Aeneas' herald came running up to the athletes, shouting, "Come, quick! The ships are burning! The women are firing the ships!"

The men turned around and saw the black cloud of smoke and ash. First to respond was Ascanius, who jumped on his horse and raced toward the beach. Approaching, he cried out, "What are you doing? My countrywomen, have you gone mad? Your future is going up in smoke!" In anger, he threw to the ground the beautiful plumed helmet he had worn at the games.

Seeing Aeneas and the other men rapidly approaching, the women scattered to the woods, afraid of their leader.

Battling the flames, which would have destroyed all the ships, Aeneas prayed to mighty Jove. The King of Gods and Men took pity on Venus' son and sent rain showers to quench the fires, saving all but four ships.

Stunned by what desperation had driven the women to do, Father Aeneas wondered whether he should abandon the rest of their voyage. Must they really go to the shores of Italy? Couldn't they establish a new Troy here in Sicily?

With night came the specter of Aeneas' dear father, Anchises, who poured out these words:

"My son, Jove has commanded me to visit you. It was he who quenched the flames with his holy showers. He says you must follow the dictates of the Fates. Take only the most determined Trojans and the mightiest warriors to Italy. You will have to fight a war against strong tribes in Latium. Leave the rest here to create a city for themselves. When you leave the shores of Sicily, you must come to the Underworld and visit me in Elysium, the Land of the Blessed. I will show you our glorious descendants, who will rule the kingdom you and Ascanius will establish in Italy."

The next morning, Aeneas gathered the weary refugees and said that anyone who wanted to stay could remain and build a great city with Acestes; those who wished to continue could follow him to their fated destination. Both groups praised his devotion to his people and the gods.

BOOK SIX

The Sibyl and the Land of the Dead

Silently, Aeneas' ships drifted into the Italian coast of Cumae. The Trojan refugees decorated the beach with up-curved sterns. Hesperia at last! The people rushed from the vessels, the men hunting game for dinner while the women started fires from the twigs and flint gathered by the children. Steadfast Aeneas selected a few of his closest companions to seek out the temple of Phoebus Apollo and the caves through which the god voiced the future.

Generations ago, the ingenious craftsman Daedalus landed here after escaping from the tower in which King Minos of Crete had imprisoned him. Daedalus had designed the king's palace at Knossos. Underneath it, he created the Labyrinth to hold the monstrous half-man, half-bull Minotaur. To keep the solution to the Labyrinth secret, Minos imprisoned the craftsman and his assistant, a son named Icarus. When Daedalus landed at Cumae, he dedicated his wings to Apollo and built a temple for the god.

Now Aeneas stared at the temple's outside walls and the murals that Daedalus had painted there:

Athenians kill a son of Minos; the grieving father prays to Zeus to avenge his son.

Athens suffers from famine and pestilence; the Oracle at Delphi pronounces a horrific remedy.

Athenian youth draw lots from a jar; the doomed tributes set sail for Crete.

The Minoan princess Ariadne falls in love with a heroic-looking youth—Theseus, the Athenian King's son.

Taking pity on the princess's longing, Daedalus reveals how Theseus can solve the Labyrinth.

A monster picks up a human's scent as a youth with a ball of string lurks in the shadows and draws his sword.

A bull's head lies in a pool of blood, severed from the body of an abomination.

Daedalus watches from a high tower as a ship full of Athenians and Ariadne sails out of a Cretan harbor.

The craftsman constructs two sets of wings from feathers and wax.

Icarus, you too would have been part of these epic panels, but a father's grief left the scene—twice attempted—incomplete in the end.

Daedalus' art entranced the visitors, and they would have spent many hours there. But Achates, who had gone ahead, returned with the Sibyl. She was a beautiful, well-kempt woman with plaited hair. After they sacrificed calves and ewes to Apollo, they followed the priestess into a cave, the back of which was honeycombed with a hundred cavernous mouths. Apollo speaks his messages through these.

Turning around to face her guests, the Sibyl looked incredibly different. Sweat beaded her pale forehead. Her now-disheveled hair stood on end, and her chest heaved with rapid breathing.

"It is time to make your request," she panted. "Phoebus Apollo, God of Prophecy, is here."

"Apollo, helper of Trojans," pious Aeneas prayed, "I beg you, tell me how I may achieve my destiny? How do I claim the land the gods have promised me?"

The god now possessed his Sibyl. Her head kept rapidly jerking from one position to the next, and in between flashed the appearance of Apollo himself. The Sibyl replied, in a voice not her own, "Son of the goddess, you have escaped the perils of the sea, but many hardships will you suffer on land. The Trojans will enter Latium, but I see war, terrible war. The Tiber runs with blood, and you will have to face an Italian Achilles. Juno will continue to plot against you, but you must not yield. Strangest of all, a Greek city will open its gates to you."

The god then left the Sibyl, and she started to recover. Aeneas then asked, "Priestess, I will face these challenges as I have faced the others. But please permit me one more request. People say that the gate to the Underworld lies in Cumae and that the dread goddess Hecate has put you in charge of it. Show me how to enter so I can once more see my father. I saved him from the Sack of Troy, carried him on my back through flames and a thousand enemy spears. Even though old age had worn him down, he traveled with us and shared our hardships for seven long years. In my dreams, his spirit visits, telling me to come to see him. Others have made the journey: Orpheus, Hercules, Theseus and Pirithous, Castor and Pollux. I am no less of a hero; I too am the child of an Olympian."

Smiling at the boast, the Cumaean Sibyl replied, "The journey is more difficult than you imagine, my friend. Pirithous and Theseus never made it back. But if you insist on descending into the gloom, you must find the Golden Bough hidden on a tree in this forest. Proserpina demands that mortals who visit bring her this gift. If the Fates allow your visit, the branch will easily break off in your hand. If not, all your strength, even if you were to use an ax, won't be able to detach it."

Venus now sent down two doves, the birds sacred to her, and they led Aeneas to the Golden Bough. He made quick work of removing it.

✳✳✳

The Sibyl led him to Lake Avernus, over which birds never flew. All night long, Aeneas and his choice companions made the necessary sacrifices. Just as the sun began to rise on a new day, the earth rumbled, the trees in the forest started to quake, and shadowy hounds howled as Hecate drew near.

"Hecate approaches!" the Sibyl rasped. "Aeneas, draw your sword and gather your courage. The rest of you, leave!" She then plunged into the cave's forbidding gloom. Aeneas followed closely behind.

Near the gate to the Underworld, they could sense but not see the forces of Disease, Hunger, and Old Age. They glimpsed bloody Discord and grim War. In the shadows, lurked centaurs, harpies, and gargoyles. The Chimaera hissed, and the Lernaean Hydra broke the surface of a nearby swamp. Seeing the three-bodied giant Geryon approaching, Aeneas raised his sword, but the Sibyl stopped his hand. "Great heroes have already killed these monsters she counseled. "What you see are their shadowy spirits."

Walking on, they reached the River Styx and saw the ancient helmsman and the decrepit barge he used to ferry spirits across these waters. The top of his head was bald, but stringy white locks fell from his temples to his shoulders. His patchy whiskers were gray, and he wore dirty rags on his time-ravaged frame. As his boat approached the shore, spirits of the dead, arms outstretched, flocked to the vessel, and the helmsman swung his long pole to frighten them away. "Who is that?" Aeneas whispered to the Sibyl. "And why won't he let those pitiful spirits onboard?"

"That," she replied, "is Charon, the grim ferryman of the dead. And those who beg for passage are spirits whose bodies lie somewhere unburied. He can't take them across."

Squinting at Aeneas, Charon asked, "What are you doing here? You're not dead, and I'm tired of taking heroes across for their evil purposes. Hercules defeated poor Cerberus and carried him trembling to the world above. Theseus and Pirithous tried to abduct Queen Proserpina from the bed of Pluto himself!"

The Sibyl replied, "Pious Aeneas is not like them. He goes to see his dear father." Then she showed him the Golden Bough, and he reluctantly let them on board. As he took them across, the boat creaked under the unaccustomed weight; Charon gave both of his passengers a dirty look. They finally reached the other side. Here, they encountered the three snarling heads of Cerberus. The Sibyl tossed three drugged honey cakes to the dog, and it quickly fell asleep.

Continuing on, Aeneas saw the spirits of infants and then the courts of the wrongly condemned. In the grove for suicides, Aeneas saw wandering among the pale trees a form he recognized. Surprised, he asked, "Dido, why are you here?" Now noticing the fresh wound in her chest, he said, "Did you do this because I left you? I swear I did not want to. The gods commanded me." But Dido refused to look at Aeneas, and soon, she returned to the arms of her loving husband, Sychaeus.

Pitying her as he went, Aeneas now came to the field for great soldiers and saw there many Trojans and Greeks continuing to fight the war. Plenty of Agamemnon's troops fled before the mighty Aeneas. He longed to talk with those beside whom he had fought—Deiphobus, Glaucus, Sarpedon—but the Sibyl warned Aeneas that it was getting late.

He now saw a dreadful citadel, from which he could hear pitiful lamentations. "Tartarus," the priestess said, "twice as far below the earth as Olympus is above. Here, the gods punish the wicked. The Titans, defeated by Jove's lightning bolt, writhe in pain. Salmoneus, who imitated the God of Thunder, was struck down, and now he suffers eternal punishment. Ixion cheated his father-in-law and then killed him. When Zeus took pity on him, Ixion tried to violate Juno. Now, the wicked man will spin forever on a fiery wheel. Theseus will always sit on a rock, unable to rise. But those who trespass against the gods aren't the only ones tortured down here. Adulterers, traitors, deserters, patricides—all those who sin against their country or their fathers also find their place in Tartarus."

✳✳✳

As the Sibyl ended her speech, they came upon the gate to Pluto's palace. Here, Aeneas fixed the Golden Bough to the door as an offering to Proserpina. Walking through, they approached the Fields of Bliss. Aeneas was amazed. Unlike the dark, gloomy places before, this grove was full of light. Aeneas looked around and saw the bright sky, green trees, and spacious meadows. Here was the best that life had to offer. Some practiced at wrestling while others reclined on their elbows and listened to poets sing about the undying glory of famous heroes. Still others delighted over their burnished weapons and sleek horses, just as they had done in life. Those who had served their country well with courage, creativity, or good deeds enjoyed this place, Elysium.

Aeneas then saw his father standing in a green valley reviewing with pride a long line of descendants yet to be born. He was contemplating their destinies and the great deeds they would perform. Seeing his beloved son striding towards him, Anchises hurried over, saying, "I knew you would come. I knew your filial devotion would see you through."

As they walked, Aeneas asked about the thousands of spirits that swarmed around a distant river. "That stream is Lethe," Anchises explained, "and the spirits around it are ones that once lived in human bodies. Having paid the price of past wrongdoings, they then drank from its waters, which has erased their memories. New identities have been assigned to them, and they wait to be reborn."

Anchises then led Aeneas and the Sibyl up a ridge to where they could see a group of these spirits. "Let me show you our descendants, great Trojans who will be born in Italy. You will marry an Italian princess named Lavinia. The child you will have with her is named Silvius, and he is at the head of this line. He will found a new city, Alba Longa. Then after him is king after king. See that one over there with the double plumes on his helmet? That is Romulus, son of the god Mars and Ilia, a descendant of ours. Under the gods' auspices, he will found Rome, a city that will rule the world!"

"What about that next group?" Aeneas asked. "Are they our Roman descendants?"

"Yes," Anchises answered. "They are descended from Ascanius Iulus. That man there is his namesake, Julius Caesar. And then the man promised to you: Augustus Caesar, the ruler who will usher in another Golden Age."

Anchises continued to point out future relatives, making his son long for the glory that was to come. Since it was nearly time to depart, he concluded by saying, "Aeneas, you are a Roman. You must crush the proud, spare the conquered, and establish peace."

Then, Anchises led his son and the Sibyl to the Gates of Sleep, after which Aeneas rejoined his men at the ships. They sailed along the coast to seek the land of Latium.

BOOK SEVEN

An Alliance Broken by Juno

Dawn, in her saffron robes, reddened the sea and brought early-morning light to gods and men. Aeneas could now make out specific features of the Italian coast. He saw vast forests, and then, at long last, he saw the great Tiber River emptying into the sea. Aeneas ordered his ships to head toward land, and all of his people shouted for joy.

Coming ashore, the refugees from Troy sought a simple meal from the forest, wild berries and other fruits that they stacked upon flatbread. Seeing how quickly everyone ate, Ascanius joked, "We're so hungry that we've even eaten our tables!"

Startled, Aeneas announced, "This is a sign. Don't you remember? The harpy Celano prophesied that our hardships would not be over until hunger drove us to eat our tables. We have arrived at the site of our homeland!" Again, all of his people cheered, and so he said, "First thing tomorrow, we will explore this area and meet its inhabitants. Today, we will sacrifice to the gods so they may have their due and we may have a feast." Taking up their bows and spears, his men went hunting in the forest while the women prepared fires from wood gathered by the children. Aeneas himself mixed wine in a large bowl.

The next day, Aeneas sent an envoy with presents and messages of peace to King Latinus. Now grown old, the King was the son of Faunus, God of the Forests and Countrysides, who in turn was a grandson of Saturn. His only heir was his daughter, Lavinia, a young woman now ready for marriage. Many of the best men in the area sought her hand, but the most handsome by far was Turnus, himself the heir of a noble line. Lavinia's mother, the Queen, desperately desired this marriage for her daughter, but the King wasn't so sure. Strange portents suggested the gods wanted a different match. Once, when Latinus and Lavinia were using a consecrated torch to light a fire at an altar, the young woman's hair caught fire, and she ran through the palace scattering holy flame. People took this to mean that her future was bright, but it would bring war to her people.

Troubled, Latinus decided to seek a message from the forest precinct of Faunus, his prophetic father. Sacrificing a hundred sheep in ritual, the King slept upon their sacred fleeces. That night, the horned god visited him in a dream. "My son, do not seek an Italian marriage for your daughter. Ignore any previous arrangements. A hero will come from foreign shores, and the child she has with him will raise our fame to the heavens. In generations to come, our descendants will rule the world!"

Now, Aeneas' embassy approached this king, who immediately offered them hospitality. "Hail, Trojans. We know about your city and the war you waged against the Greeks. We have heard of your heroes and the Fall of Troy. You are a people from our own stock since your founder, Dardanus, came from this peninsula. As long as I am the king, you shall not want. So, tell me your purpose. What brings you to our shores?"

The oldest of the Trojans, Ilioneus, now stepped forward. "King Latinus, the gods bring us to your city walls. We ask only for a strip of land where we may build a home for Troy's penates. To assure you of our peaceful intentions, our king, the great hero Aeneas, sends these gifts, treasures rescued from Troy: a majestic robe and crown used by Priam himself."

While Ilioneus spoke, Latinus brooded upon his daughter's marriage and the message he had received from Father Faunus. He then replied, "We graciously accept these gifts as signs of peace and long to meet your King Aeneas. The gods have told me to marry my daughter, Lavinia, to a hero who arrives from another land. Their union will raise our people's fame to the skies. Together, the Latins and the Trojans will produce these people destined for greatness."

✳✳✳

Returning from Argos, Juno looked down from her golden chariot and noticed Aeneas' ships at the mouth of the Tiber. The Trojans had reached Italy! They had even begun building an outpost, earthen walls surrounding a cleared field. She was furious. "I will have to concede that Aeneas will marry Lavinia and rule Latium. I cannot overturn Fate, but I can delay it, and I can make both the Trojans and Latins suffer along the way."

She now called on the most feared of the Furies: Allecto, the Dread Goddess of War and Wrath. "Daughter of Pluto and Night, you know how to cause strife and bloodshed. Bring about a war between the Trojans and Latins. May the dowry for Lavinia's marriage be the blood and gore of battle. Let Bellona be her matron of honor."

As frightful as a Gorgon, Allecto shot up from Hell and sped to Latium. Arriving at the room of Queen Amata, the Fury took a black snake from her own hair and let it writhe into her victim's heart. Its venom inflamed the Queen's anger over the canceled wedding to Turnus.

Now, like a Maenad, Amata ran through the streets, waving torches and calling all the mothers to join her. "If you care for a mother's rights, then leave your homes, let down your hair, and rave with me in response to this injustice. Come, celebrate the revels of Bacchus." The women responded to her call. Husbands and sons watched helplessly, knowing better than to interfere with women caught up in the ecstasy of the Wine God's strange rites.

Pleased with her work here, Allecto now flew to Ardea. She found Turnus sound asleep, so she transformed from a terrifying Fury to an old woman, a priestess at Juno's temple. So disguised, she appeared to him in a dream. "Turnus, why are you sleeping? Don't you know a foreigner has usurped your high standing in Latinus' opinion and even now is seeking Lavinia for his bride? Juno commands you to burn their ships and kill them all!"

In his dream, Turnus sneered, "Go away, old woman. I know what's what. Let me decide matters of war and peace.

Stick with guarding the idols in Juno's temple. I don't need you stirring up panic."

These words enraged Allecto. Now, her appearance changed. Asps grew from her scalp and writhed in her unkempt hair. Black clothes dripped like oil down her body. As she spoke in reply, her snakes hissed at him. "See here, mortal. Now, do I look like an old busy-body to you? I am Allecto, one of the Furies, and I come from Hell bearing war and death." Then, taking up a torch, she reared back and threw it into his chest. Turnus awoke, screaming. He called his men to arms.

One more thing and the war would begin. Allecto flew to the forest where Aeneas' son, Ascanius, was hunting. She caused his dogs to pick up the scent of a majestic, tame stag, loved by the Latins. Not knowing the animal's importance, Ascanius nocked an arrow and released the taut bow. The arrow zipped through the air and into the side of the stag, taking its life. Allecto spread the rumor of what happened. Country folk picked up clubs, axes, whatever could serve rage as a weapon. The Fury flew to a high point, took up a shepherd's horn, and sounded a call that caused men to pour in from every part of the countryside. She inflamed their lust for violence and death.

The Trojans snatched up their armor, swords, and spears and rushed out of their camp to help Ascanius. Battle lines formed. Soldiers slipped in blood. Bodies littered the field. This was no country brawl. This was the beginning of war.

People began to mob the Latin palace, screaming "Murder!" From the battlefield, men carried the bodies of their brothers; fathers carried the bodies of their sons. Turnus, a head taller than any other man, demanded that they drive the newcomers from Italian soil. Through it all, King Latinus remained unmoved. He refused to engage in blasphemous violence. But he also recognized that he was powerless to stop it. So, he locked himself in the palace. Juno herself had to throw open the Gates of Janus.

BOOK EIGHT

The Shield of Aeneas

Thankful that Ascanius had escaped from the village battle, Aeneas was still troubled by the rumors of war. Only days ago, he had allied with King Latinus, who promised marriage to Lavinia. Now, the Latins, the Rutulians, and all the surrounding tribes were sharpening spears, banging on shields, and forming into ranks, ready to wipe out the Trojans.

"How is this possible?" he asked his companion-in-arms Achates. "Why would Latinus turn on us over a dead stag?"

"He doesn't want this war, but he is no longer in control. The people follow someone named Turnus. He is King of the Rutulians."

That night, Aeneas fell into a troubled sleep. Rising from the depths of the hero's mind, Father Tiber flowed into a dream. His hair was green reeds, and his beard was blond rolling water. His blue robes flowed down his body and ended in white sediment from the mountains. "Son of the goddess, I have waited a long time for you to come, to build your homeland on my banks, a homeland that will rule the world! So, do not give up, Aeneas. Jove, who is always allied with the Fates, has not changed his mind. Do not fear war. You will triumph." The old river god went on to tell him to join with King Evander and his Arcadians, who had come from Greece to the Palatine Hill in Italy. "These people," he said, "are perpetually at war with the Latins and will fight to the death for you." After telling Aeneas how to reach these allies, Father Tiber revealed a sign he would send.

The next morning, with a renewed sense of purpose, Aeneas chose two ships from his fleet and picked out the crews. Before sailing, he saw the sign: a white sow and her thirty piglets. Pious Aeneas then sacrificed the sow to Juno, hoping that she would give up her hatred of the Trojans.

They sailed up the Tiber for a full day before finding the citadel of the Arcadians. From the ships, he could see a large group of people outside the city walls; they were making a sacrifice at the Great Altar of Hercules. The Arcadian king's brave son, the godlike Pallas, bravely strode up to the ships with a spear in his hand and confronted the Trojans. "Who are you? What is your purpose? Are you here for peace or war?"

Aeneas held out an olive branch and replied, "We are refugees from the Sack of Troy, and we are at war with the Latins. We have come to seek King Evander's armed help. Tell him the ancestors of Dardanus wish to speak to him."

Hearing this, Pallas immediately welcomed them and invited them to the feast. King Evander not only knew about the Trojans, whom he called Dardanians, and their war with the Greeks, but he also had fond memories of Priam and Anchises visiting Acadia. "They were both my guest-friends when I lived in Greece, and I will gladly show you hospitality for their sake." With that, King Evander, stooped with old age, led Aeneas around the citadel, which would one day become the site of Rome.

***

Venus worried about Aeneas' upcoming war against Turnus. That night, she paid a rare visit to the bedroom of her ugly husband, Vulcan, the great blacksmith to the gods. Sitting next to him, Venus dropped her chin and looked up at her husband and said, "You know, I never asked you to arm my Trojans when they were fighting the Greeks, not even when I saw the immortal armor you made Thetis for her son, Achilles. Now, my poor Aeneas will have to fight the Rutulians and Latins to get the land fated to him. Dearest, please use your divine art to make my son the tools of war: helmet and sword, shield and breastplate. Then I could turn a mother's worry into a wife's gratitude." No one, not even a god, can resist Venus' immortal words of love. The next morning, Vulcan hobbled to his forge under Mount Aetna and created masterpieces for his wife's son.

King Evander also rose early. He found Aeneas anxious to finalize the terms of their alliance. "Son of the Goddess and last hope of the mighty Trojans," the King began, "we Arcadians are few and cannot offer you enough help. I want to connect you to a nearby kingdom, a powerful one that is at odds with Turnus. Long ago, Lydians founded a city in the Tuscan mountains. These Etruscans prospered until an evil tyrant came to power—Mezentius, who butchered his own people. His favorite torture was to bind a living man to a corpse—hand to hand, mouth to mouth until his victim died in putrefaction."

"You don't propose that I work with him, do you?" a shocked Aeneas asked.

"No, no, no. The Etruscans rose up in rebellion. Mezentius managed to escape, and Turnus now protects him. These people are ready to go to war against the Rutulians and are only held back by a seer, who tells them they must await a foreign leader. Aeneas, you will lead these thousands.

"Furthermore," Evander continued, "I will give you two hundred of my best warriors and entrust you with my pride and joy, my only son, Pallas. Let him learn the art of war from you and hold you in awe."

Suddenly, thunder rumbled, and lightning flashed through the clear blue sky. The heavens resounded with Tuscan horns and clashing arms. Full of awe and dread, the people cowered—all except Aeneas, who knew this was a sign of divine approval from his mother.

After gathering some of his finest Trojans and sending the rest back to Ascanius, Aeneas rode at the head of the cavalry, with Pallas commanding the middle of the line.

✳✳✳

Shining as brightly as the Morning Star, the heavenly body most sacred to her, Venus appeared in the sky proudly carrying Aeneas' new armor, wonders crafted by Vulcan. When she found her son alone by a stream, watering his horse, she made herself visible to him. She welcomed Aeneas' embrace and then laid the gifts at his feet before transforming herself again into a divine brightness in the morning sky. Awestruck, Aeneas warily picked up the fearsome helmet with plumes the color of fire. He tested the sword and noted its perfect balance and heft. He put on the bronze breastplate, blood-red in color. And then he saw the greatest wonder of all, the shield with its ineffable designs. On its surface, Vulcan had embossed prophecies: the future of Italy and Rome's greatest triumphs, the generations that sprang from young Iulus and all the wars they fought:

A she-wolf lies on the banks of the Tiber, and twin boys nurse fearlessly at her teats.

Followers of Romulus snatch Sabine women from the crowd watching the horse races in the Circus.

The sons of Romulus fight an epic war with Tatius; suddenly, the Sabine women intervene and convince both sides to reconcile.

Next, the same kings stand before Jove's altar and make a treaty over a sacrificed sow.

Lars Porsenna, the Etruscan King, wages war against Rome to restore the exiled Tarquin.

Gauls lie in ambush outside the gates of Rome. Their hair is gold, and their necks are milk-white against the darkness of night. A silver goose honks out a warning.

Next, the twelve Salii, the leaping priests of Mars, dance and sing in procession around the city. Each wears a spiked headdress and wields a sacred shield.

Most magnificent of all, though, was the center of the shield, where a sea battle raged on silver waves tipped with golden foam. Augustus Caesar defeats the Egyptian ships of Antony and Cleopatra. He returns to Rome triumphant.

Aeneas could not understand the meaning of the prophecies he saw on the shield, but with reverence and pride, he carried the glorious destiny of his children.

BOOK NINE

Nisus and Euryalus

A rainbow appeared in the sky, and Iris suddenly stood before Turnus, bearing a message from Juno. "Now is the time to attack the Trojan camp. Aeneas has gone to seek allies among the Etruscans, and he has taken his best men with him. What are you waiting for?" With that, Iris streaked back through the sky in all her pretty colors.

Turnus marshaled his Rutulian troops, and they advanced across the plain. "Their fortification is only a mound of dirt topped with a wooden fence," he called to his men. "This will be the second Fall of Troy!"

***

One of the Trojan sentries saw with his skilled eyes a smudge moving on the horizon. He immediately knew what it was and sounded the alarm. Trojans outside the gates rushed back. Aeneas had left orders that if the Latins attacked before he returned, no one was to fight outside the fortifications.

Now, Turnus rode far ahead of his troops. Arriving at the gates, he issued a challenge. "Cowards! Why are you hiding inside your flimsy walls? Come out and fight like men!" When no one appeared, he rode around the camp, looking for a way inside, but found none. He roared in frustration, and then screamed to his men, "Fire the ships!"

Waving a flaming brand above his head, he inspired his men to do the same. They rode toward the beach. But just as Turnus reared back to fling his torch at the ships, a blinding light flashed through the heavens. The voice of the Great Mother spoke for all to hear, filling both Latins and Trojans with awe and dread. "Turnus, how dare you violate these ships? They are mine!"

After the Sack of Troy, Cybele, the Great Mother, went to her son, Jove, as a suppliant and asked, "From time immemorial, there has been a grove of pines on Mount Ida that is sacred to me, a place where I have received many offerings. I gladly yield these trees to Aeneas so he can build his ships and lead the Trojan refugees to their glorious destiny. Grant that these ships will never fail since I, mother of the gods, make this sacrifice to humans."

Jove, who marshalls the storm clouds, looked troubled. "Should things made by man be immortal and infallible? No, but I will do this: I will take those ships that survive the journey, that anchor on Italy's coast, and transform them into beautiful sea nymphs."

While Turnus' men were still blinking, the ships pulled away from the shore and dove prow-first beneath the waves. They breached the surface in the forms of young girls breasting the sea.

"Go forth, my sea goddesses," cried the Great Mother. "You are now free!"

Turnus' frustration threatened to turn to anger, but only for a moment. "Look, men!" he laughed. "Even their ships are afraid of us. This is a good omen. The gods themselves have cut off the Trojans' means of escape." At these words, the men cheered and shook their spears.

Having steeled his men for battle, Turnus then announced, "Make camp here. We attack at dawn."

***

Young Iulus consulted with the elder soldier Mnestheus while the Trojans prepared to defend their walls of dirt and wood. They gathered the most massive rocks and hauled them to the gangways. Archers double-checked the soundness of their bows and sharpened their arrows. After testing the gates, they reinforced weaknesses and set the watchmen with the keenest eyes.

At one post stood Nisus, a fierce warrior and loyal companion to Aeneas. Euryalus was there too. He was younger, a beard just beginning to show on his cheeks. No youth in Aeneas' army was more handsome. The two were inseparable, and one love bound them.

"Euryalus, I am so restless; I can't just stand guard. I must do something, especially since the Latins out there are asleep and the Rutulians are drunk."

"Nisus, they too have sentries, who are as alert as we are. I know you are always as ready for battle as Mars is, but there will be plenty of opportunity for glory in the morning."

"But listen. Here's what I'm thinking. We need Aeneas and the reinforcements he sought. I am known for stealth, so I could sneak through the enemy's camp. Look, there's a path I could take. I could then alert Aeneas, and he'd be here to save us."

"Nisus, what makes you think I'd let you go by yourself? I crave glory as much as you do. And you could use another set of eyes."

"Euryalus, I know how well you fought after Ascanius killed the Latins' deer and they were thirsty for his blood. But some god may take your life during such a venture, and I would never want to bring grief to your dear mother. She's the only soldier's mother to follow Aeneas on the final leg of his journey, so we all owe her great respect."

"My mind is made up. You are not undertaking this risk alone. Grab your weapons. We need to speak to Ascanius."

Nisus and Euryalus found young Iulus in council with Mnestheus and the other elder soldiers. Nervous about interrupting the meeting, they nevertheless voiced their idea.

Ascanius replied, "I would greatly reward such an undertaking, and you both would be my dearest companions."

Euryalus then timidly added, "Ascanius who has become Iulus, if we do not return, please take care of my mother. She forfeited the safety of Acestes' city rather than leave me, and now I leave her ignorant of this venture; I could not bear to see her cry and beg me to stay."

The son of Aeneas replied, "Of course. She will become my dear mother, lacking only the name Creusa." With tears in his eyes after seeing such devotion in a son, Ascanius handed his sword to Euryalus for good luck.

The two friends set out. Once they reached the camp, Nisus whispered to his young companion, "Euryalus, now is the time for me to cut a path through these drunkards. Watch my back."

As Nisus stabbed those soldiers lying on the ground and cut off the drooping heads of those that were sitting, Euryalus walked backward but soon began to kill Rutulians as well. The companions now came to the great Messapus' camp, with all its riches. But Nisus said, "We've killed enough for now. Let's get going before the morning is here."

Euryalus grabbed Messapus' golden helmet with its thick plumes, put it on, and found it almost covered his eyes. He then ran to catch up with Nisus. But now came the Latin cavalry, riding out to join the Rutulian army before the attack at dawn. Euryalus was cut off from his friend, and the riders spotted the plundered helmet, gleaming in Dawn's pale first light.

Assuming the youth was right behind him, Nisus ran as fast as he could and got away. When he paused to catch his breath, he looked around for Euryalus, but could not find him anywhere. Back through the thick woods, trying to retrace his steps, Nisus desperately searched for his companion. But then he heard clanging and shouts. He looked in that direction and saw the bloodthirsty cavalry bearing down on his terrified friend. Rushing to help him, regardless of the odds, Nisus sent forth winged words of prayer, "Diana, Goddess of the Hunt, if my sacrifices ever pleased you, guide my spear and let it break up that swarm." He threw, and the spear nicked a few horsemen before punching through the chest of one of the Latin captains. Nisus readied his next spear, took aim at the scattering troops, and threw. This one went through another captain's temple and rested in the man's cloven brain.

Furious that he could not find who threw the spears, the general drew his sword and moved toward Euryalus. This was too much for Nisus, who broke cover and ran into the regrouping cavalry, desperate to save his friend. But just as the general's sword cut through the youth's ribs and left a bloody swath across the hairless chest, several horsemen arrested Nisus and ended his scream by hacking his head from his body.

✳✳✳

When Turnus arrived on the scene and took stock of the Rutulian dead, he ordered the heads of Nisus and Euryalus put on stakes, which he then had two of his soldiers take up. He formed his battalions behind them, and they proceeded to march around the Trojans' walls.

Seeing the gory heads they knew so well, the soldiers on the ramparts could only gape in silent grief. The news reached Euryalus' mother, who tore her hair, raked her nails down her face, and beat her breast while letting loose lamentations that chilled everyone around her. She rushed to the gangways, pushed aside soldiers who tried to bar her from the Latins' gruesome trophies, and screamed. She sang out, "Euryalus, the only one that the invading Greeks left to me. Husband, gone. All the beautiful children I bore, gone—all except you, who was to be a comfort to me in my old age. So I followed you for all these years, just to be close to you, the only one left for me to love. Turnus, if you have any decency, any respect for an old woman, you will let me bury my son. If you don't, then direct all your men to throw their spears at me."

Listening to her lament, the soldiers next to her wept. Ascanius and the elders with him directed a couple of soldiers to lead her gently away.

***

The siege began in earnest. The Volscians, those troops from the area south of Latium, arranged themselves in the tortoise formation, creating ranks covered by shields in front and on top. Then, they moved into the trench that surrounded the Trojan fortification so other troops could march over their comrades' raised shields. But the Trojans had a lot of experience defending city walls. Archers picked off those crossing the trench. Then the Trojans rolled a monstrous boulder over the top of the wall, which crushed the center of the Volscian shell and scattered its remaining members.

Those who had crossed the trenches and avoided Trojan arrows now tore down the wooden barriers and rushed toward the city walls. Messapus called for ladders, and Rutulians began to climb. At the top of the fortifications, Trojans used long pikes to push the ladders away. But now the Italians appeared with torches and hurled them at a tower connected to the walls by gangways. The men trapped inside panicked and ran from one side to another, attempting to avoid the flames. Suddenly, the tower collapsed. The men inside were crushed by its weight and impaled on the splinters.

The Italians cheered and continued to fill the trench with earth and to attack the walls. Seeing one Rutulian approach the gate with a flaming torch, Ilioneus, one of the Trojan captains, laid him low with a huge craggy rock, the kind that nowadays not even two men could lift. When Mezentius spotted an archer aiming down at a Volscian, he whirled his slingshot several times over his head and launched a stone that split the Trojan's skull.

Numanus Remulus, Turnus' new brother-in-law, strutted towards the wall, boasting of Rutulian prowess. "Do you Trojans ever fight like men? Or do you always hide behind walls? There's no Achilles here for you to be afraid of, no Ulysses to dupe you. We put helmets on our sons' heads when they're little boys and make them fight their enemies in hand-to-hand combat. But when you Trojans are attacked, you hide your boys, even the great Aeneas' son, with the women. We expose ourselves to the elements to show how tough we are, while you guys wear saffron robes and tunics with sleeves so your arms ..." An arrow punched through Numanus' throat, turning the final words on his lips into blood. Ascanius, tired of the man's boasting, had nocked an arrow, prayed to Jove, and made his first shot as a warrior. Cheers went up along the Trojan gangways.

Looking down from Olympus, Apollo, God of the Silver Bow, nodded his approval but feared young Iulus would grow over-confident and get killed. He shot himself down to earth and transformed into the elder Butes, who had been Anchises' armor-bearer. He approached the boy and said, "Great shot, Ascanius! But be satisfied with this auspicious beginning to your career as a warrior. Apollo himself must be proud of you. But you are still too young for war, and too much depends upon your survival." As the counterfeit Butes finished, he shot into the air. The soldiers around Iulus knew that a god had visited the boy; they could hear the god's arrows clang inside his quiver as he flew away. Therefore, they led Aeneas' great son to safety.

Now Pandarus and Bitias, Trojan sons of a wood nymph on Mount Ida, opened the main gate and, in its doorway, stood tall and proud, like twin pines on the banks of a river. Straightaway, Italians rushed the opening, but only to be cut down or scared off by the two brothers. Other Trojan soldiers grew bold as well, venturing farther and farther outside the gates to engage the enemy.

Turnus appeared. He first engaged with Antiphates, son of the great warrior Sarpedon, a son of Jove. Turnus hurled his mighty spear. It tunneled into Antiphates' chest and lodged in his left lung; blood foamed around the fatal wound. The King of the Rutulians killed several more before engaging with Bitias. He grabbed a pike lying on the ground and launched it at the giant. Bitias raised his shield but to no avail. Turnus hurled the pike with such force that it bored through the shield and cuirass and perforated Bitias' heart. He fell like a giant pine in the forest, knocking down several of its companions before hitting the ground.

When Pandarus saw his brother crumple to the ground, he knew the tide had turned and quickly closed the gates. He trapped several Trojans outside the walls, but accidentally enclosed Turnus with them, like a hungry wolf in a sheep pen. When the Trojans recognized that hateful face, that massive body, they panicked, all except Pandarus, who sought revenge for his brother's death.

"You're dead," Pandarus yelled at the Rutulian king. "This isn't Queen Amata's bedroom you've snuck into. You're in the enemy camp, and there's no escape."

A wicked smile spread over Turnus' face. "That's good. You should run along and tell your king that another Achilles is here."

Pandarus threw his spear with perfect aim, but Juno deflected it. Turnus leapt and brought his sword down on the giant's head, splitting the Trojan's face in two. The earth shook from the impact of Pandarus' colossal body.

Turnus was so full of blood lust that he never thought to open the gates and let his army stream in. Juno filled the Rutulian king with courage and doubled his strength. Berserk, he took down Trojan after Trojan, grabbing spears on the run as he cut a gorry path through the camp.

When word of the slaughter reached the senior captains, they ran to the scene and found their soldiers scattered. "Where are you men going?" they yelled. "Do you have other walls to protect you? He's trapped in here with us, and we outnumber him! Turn and fight!"

These words filled the men with courage, and they ran full tilt at the Rutulian king. With all the missiles raining down on him, Turnus knew he could not hold up much longer. His shield barely held together. His helmet was split, and the horsehair crest was lost. He climbed the wall that bordered the river. Bleeding from several severe wounds, Turnus leapt from the wall and dove headfirst into the Tiber below. The current bore him to the arms of his anxious men.

BOOK TEN

The Return of Aeneas

D espite chasing Turnus from their stronghold, the Trojans were still desperate for help. Only the arrows of expert archers kept Rutulians from torching the wooden walls. Latins pressed at every gate. Brothers of the great Sarpedon of Lycia threw down massive boulders, the kind two men, such as mortals are nowadays, could scarcely lift. But ammunition of this sort was in short supply.

Looking down from his celestial throne, Jove noticed the battle around the Trojans' stronghold. Storm clouds gathered along his brow, and he called his Olympians into council.

Noticing the lightning flashing in the King's eyes, the other gods sat in silence. After a while, Jove spoke. "I told you all that I did not want Italy and Troy to go to war. Yet I look down and see Turnus commanding Rutulian and Latin forces against a poorly defended Trojan outpost. You knew it was my will, which is always allied with the Fates, that the Italians welcome

Aeneas. What has caused this hate and violence? Soon enough, Hannibal will lead his Carthaginians across the Alps and bring war to Italian soil. There's no reason to hasten bloody conflict."

Venus began, "Dear Father, mightiest of all immortals, all I know is what I see: Turnus, swollen with pride, riding around in his chariot and sending wave after wave of Rutulians against a Trojan homeland still in its infancy. And of course, this happens while Aeneas and his best men are forming alliances with other tribes in Italy. In seeking Italy, have the Trojan's defied your will or misinterpreted the Fates' decree? If so, then let the fledgling city fail, let the Trojans go extinct, though it would have been far better for Aeneas to die gloriously defending Priam's city. But if the refugees are following your will in establishing a new homeland in Latium, then I don't see why Juno gets to usurp so much power. She marshals the storm clouds and commands the sea to sack Troy's ships. She sends Iris to incite the Trojan women to burn the ships. She opens the gates of Hades and sends forth into the world a Fury. It seems to me that she is trying to spin a new fate for Italy."

Queen Juno was fuming. "So, I'm to blame for all this? Who told Aeneas he had to fight the Latins? Not me. Who told him to stir up the Arcadians or to put a boy in charge while he went to make alliances? Aeneas did those things himself. Who told him to take a bride already promised to another and thus make an enemy of Turnus? Venus, I believe you did. Not that I care for Turnus. He's a nobody, and his mother is nothing but a minor goddess. And whose fault is it that the Trojan people are so few? Is it mine? Or is it loverboy Paris' fault and yours for encouraging him to bring Helen—and thus a thousand Greek ships—to Troy?"

When Juno finished, the other Olympians started talking among themselves, arguing one side or the other. Meanwhile, Jove brooded. Finally, he announced, "Venus, Juno, since you two can't get along, here's my decree, and everyone better take it to heart and remember it. Neither I nor any other Olympian shall interfere in the war between the Italians and the Trojans. Whatever the humans decide to do, the Fates will find their way." That brought an end to the discussion. Jove rose from his golden throne and left the hall, followed by the other gods and goddesses.

✳✳✳

As the Trojans struggled to defend their stronghold, Aeneas was leading an armada across the midnight sea. After leaving King Evander, Venus' son had sped to the Tuscan camp and presented himself and his cause. Tarchon, the leader of the Etruscans, immediately recognized the fulfillment of the prophecy and submitted his army to a foreign general.

Thirty ships carrying the Trojan embassy, the Arcadian allies, and thousands of Etruscan soldiers cut through the dark water. Throughout the night, steadfast Aeneas remained wide-awake and handled the tiller. Then, a miracle! In front of the ships, sea nymphs danced. Their leader put her hands on the stern and looked in Aeneas' eyes. "Don't you recognize us?" she said with a sly smile. "We are the ships that you beached on the shores of Italy. When Turnus threatened to set us on fire, Cybele, the Great Mother, had Jove transform us into the forms you see before you."

Aeneas, awestruck, asked, "Is the camp under attack?"

"It is," she replied. "We have been swimming throughout the sea to find you. Latins, Rutulians, and Volscians have crossed the trench. Now, they beat at the gates and threaten to fire the wooden walls and towers. You must hurry and storm the beaches by morning. Young Ascanius is counting on you." And with that, she gave the ship a mighty push that sent it speeding across the waves.

✳✳✳

When the shore was in sight, Tarchon spread this order to all his ships: "Row with all your strength. Plow the beaches with the bronze prows of your ships!" The loyal soldiers arched their backs as they pulled on the oars.

When Dawn rose and stretched her pink light across land and sea, Turnus saw the ships coming. Undeterred, he shouted to his men, "Aeneas expects to get the jump on us. Just as Trojan spears welcomed a thousand ships from Greece, Italy shall meet their landing parties at the water's edge. Fortune favors the bold!"

As Rutulian and Latin troops raced to the beach, Aeneas leapt from the bow of his ship before it even left the water. His god-forged armor blazed in the morning sun.

Aeneas attacked first, cutting a crimson path through Latin troops. On came the sons of Melampus, a companion to Hercules during his labors. But the clubs they swung were no help to them now. Next, the brothers of Cydon launched seven spears at the son of the goddess, which his helmet and shield stopped. He turned and yelled to Achates, "Keep feeding me those spears. They tasted Greek blood on the plains of Troy. Now, I'll bury them in Latin flesh!" The next one flew like a javelin straight through the air and punched through Maeon's shield and corslet before perforating his heart.

On another front, Pallas spotted his Arcadians running from the Latin troops. He called out to them, "Friends, who are you running from? You're not fighting gods. These are mortal men. And where do you plan to run to? We have the sea at our backs." Pallas then charged, cutting down one enemy after another. His first victim had been bending down to lift a massive stone. Pallas' spear went into the man's spine. On the run, Pallas pulled the spear from the corpse and threw it at the man's companion, who had hoped to avenge his friend's death. Blood foamed around the wound made in the man's chest. Next, Pallas squared off against twin brothers. Using King Evander's sword, he cut off the head of the first and the hand of the second. Its fingers were still clasping a sword when it hit the ground. Pallas' brave deeds steeled the hearts of the Arcadians, who rallied and followed him into battle.

But Pallas' success caught the attention of Lausus, the son of the ousted King Mezentius. Now, he began cutting a bloody path to King Evander's son. Of equal age and ability, the two men prepared to confront one another. But they didn't square off. Each was fated to fall to a much greater adversary, and soon.

The nymph Juturna now warned her brother, Turnus, that young Lausus was in trouble. Jumping onto his waiting chariot, he plowed a path between his troops and Aeneas'. He called out, "Everyone, back off! Pallas is mine to kill. I only wish his father were here to watch."

Shocked by the arrogant disrespect, Pallas replied, "Today, the glory is mine. Either I take your armor as spoils or die fighting bravely. My father is strong enough to handle whichever course the Fates have planned." The son of Evander then strode to the middle of the field.

Handing the reins to his charioteer, Turnus leapt from the back of his moving chariot; the ground trembled when his massive form landed. Pallas ran toward the Rutulian chieftain, praying as he raised his weapon. "Hercules, son of almighty Jove, remember the annual rites my father celebrated at your Great Altar and guide my spear to victory. Let Turnus watch as I rip the armor from his dying body."

On Olympus, Hercules heard the young man and groaned. He knew the Fates would not allow him to save the son of his friend. Jove turned to him and said, "Every mortal must die, and brief is the time granted to any man. Yet glorious deeds win fame, which lengthens the impact of a hero's life."

When he was within range, Pallas threw his spear. It hit the top of Turnus' shield and nicked his shoulder. The massive Rutulian shrugged and said, "Now, let's see if mine can go a little deeper," and with that, he reared back and launched his own weapon. It hit the center of Pallas' shield, boring through several layers of bronze and oxhide before punching through the corslet and cutting into the young man's heart. Pallas pulled the spear from his body, but then fell to the ground, a corpse.

Standing above his victim, Turnus shouted, "Arcadians, take Pallas' body and give him a hero's funeral. May that comfort the boy's father. Evander had to pay dearly for helping Aeneas." With that, Turnus put his foot on Pallas' corpse and wrenched away the belt, a work of art, and exulted in the spoils.

Looking down from Olympus, Jove turned again to Hercules and said, "Man cannot see the doom right in front of him. Soon, Turnus will rue the day he exacted such a price from Evander, King of the Arcadians."

***

When word of Pallas' death reached Aeneas, grief, guilt, and rage coursed through him. Now, Aeneas raced toward Turnus like a torrent overwhelming everything in its path. He aimed his spear at Magnus, who ducked and cowered at the Trojan's knees and pleaded, "Accept me as a suppliant and spare my life. The masses of gold in my house shall be yours." But Aeneas grasped Magnus' helmet, pulled back his head, and submerged his sword up to the hilt in the suppliant's neck. Next, he took four men alive to sacrifice at Pallas' funeral.

Tarquitus, son of Faunus and a nymph, challenged Aeneas, who threw his spear through the man's shield, charged, and cut off his head without a trace of pity. "Lie there. Your mother will never perform your funeral rites. Instead, I'll leave you for the vultures." These were just a few of the dead Aeneas left in his wake.

High on Olympus, Jove, who had been watching the progress of the battle, now turned to his wife and said, "Well Juno, the Trojans seem to be doing much better now that Aeneas and his allies have arrived."

Teary-eyed, Juno replied, "Please don't mock me right now, when I am sick at heart over Turnus' impending death. I want to help him, but you made it clear that none of us are to interfere. I'm terrified of the punishment you would give me. I know the Fates have determined that Turnus must die, but if you love me, then allow me to save his life for a little while, long enough for him to see his dear father again."

Jove was suspicious, but replied, "If you sincerely understand that Turnus must die and that this reprieve cannot change the course of the war, then you can postpone his death."

Juno didn't wait to hear more. Mounting her golden chariot, she drove through the clouds and arrived at the scene of battle. There, she created a phantom Aeneas and set him down near Turnus. The counterfeit challenged the Rutulian general, who then threw his spear. When it missed, the fake Aeneas turned and ran.

Laughing and shouting taunts, Turnus pursued him onto a nearby ship, believing he had the foreigner cornered. But as soon as the Rutulian boarded, Juno cut the mooring ropes and pushed the vessel out to sea. When he saw Aeneas vanish and noticed he was floating away, Turnus looked up to the heavens and cried, "Gods, why do you do this to me? So many men followed me into battle, and they will think that I have abandoned them. From now on, they will call me a coward." Three times Turnus tried to jump overboard so he could swim back to land, but each time, Juno stopped him. The tide bore him back to his city and the arms of his father.

***

The absence of Turnus emboldened the Trojans and their allies. They now surged forward in the hope of winning the war once and for all. But the ousted King Mezentius charged into the fray. He caught one man in the face with a massive shard of granite. He hamstrung another and left him to bleed out. Then he killed Mimas. The same age as Trojan Paris, the two had been constant companions as boys. Now, Paris' ashes mingle with the soil of his fatherland while Mimas' corpse rests in an unmarked grave on Italy's shore.

The Etruscans moved to the front. They hated their former king, and many of them had lost fathers to his horrific tortures. Though they longed for revenge, they dared not get too close. When a boar, driven from his mountain home by dogs, reaches a group of hunters, it snorts and raises its hackles. No man dares come close; each throws his spear from a safe distance. Undaunted, the boar shakes their shafts from its back and bares its tusks at each of its opponents. So too Mezentius faced off against troops who stood well back.

Even the mighty Orodes, seeing his comrade fall, turned and ran. Refusing to kill a man in such a cowardly fashion, Mezentius swiftly caught up with Orodes. After besting him in hand-to-hand combat, Mezentius cried out in triumph and planted his boot on the man's chest to pull out his spear. With his dying breath, Orodes said, "You won't gloat for long. My fate will be yours. Soon, my avenger will come and, for all your fighting spirit, destroy you and your reckless pride."

Aeneas, still seeking revenge for Pallas' death, now saw his soldiers fleeing the massive form of Mezentius, who like the giant hunter Orion, pursued his prey without fear. The two men now squared off against each other. Mezentius threw his spear, but Aeneas' shining shield, with its images of a future Rome, easily deflected it. Now, it was Aeneas' turn. He reared back and launched his spear with all his might. It hit and punched through the several layers of bronze and leather before piercing Mezentius' groin.

Aeneas charged forward, flashing his god-made sword. Just as he was about to bring it down on his injured prey, Mezentius' son, Lausus, dove between the two men and parried the blow meant for his dear father. The devoted son held back Aeneas so his father could escape. Then, a swarm of Rutulian spears and arrows came down on the son of the goddess, but the gifts of Vulcan protected him. "Lausus," he yelled, "you are a fool. You cannot hope to withstand me. Your filial piety blinds you to the black doom hanging over your head." Aeneas continued to threaten the young man, who would not back down. Enraged, Aeneas stabbed his sword through Lausus shield and corslet; the blade punctured his heart.

Looking down at the corpse, Aeneas regretted what he had done, and his killing frenzy left him. Kneeling, he said, "Keep your armor. I take no trophies from you." He then called forth the Rutulians to take Lausus' body back to his father.

Mezentius was cleaning his wound in the Tiber's water when his soldiers carried to him his son's corpse. Torn by feelings of grief and guilt, he mounted his horse and took off after Aeneas. Ravaged by the pain his ride caused, he still managed to roar, "Trojan, you have hurt me in the only possible way. You have killed my son." In rapid succession, he launched three spears, but the god-forged shield protected Venus' son.

Then it was Aeneas' turn. He felled Mezentius' horse, which pinned its rider underneath. Looking up at the man who killed his son, the ousted king whispered, "Goddess-born Aeneas, finish me. I long to die. Permit me one final request. The Etruscans hate me and rightfully so. They will avenge their loved ones on my corpse. Make sure my body lies in the same tomb as my son's." Mezentius did not flinch when Aeneas' sword came down upon him. He breathed out his spirit, which traveled to the shades below.

BOOK ELEVEN

Camilla

Reluctantly, Dawn left the side of Tithonus, put on her saffron robes, and spread her rose-colored light so weary mortals could resume their labor. Tired and depressed, pious Aeneas longed to grieve for Pallas, but as the victor of yesterday's contest, he had sacred duties to perform. The son of the goddess gathered Mezentius' armor and brought it to a high hill that overlooked the battlefield. He erected the trunk of a large oak and clothed it in Mezentius' helmet and breastplate. He stood the shield and spear at the base. Then, he gathered his men.

Looking out on the crowd of exhausted soldiers, Aeneas gathered all his energy and said, "This morning we gather to show our gratitude to Mars, God of War. We offer up these spoils taken from the mighty and evil Mezentius. Tomorrow, we march on Latium and take what its king promised us. Today, we bury our dead."

With his people starting to build funeral pyres, Aeneas could now give in to his grief for Pallas. Approaching the young man's corpse, the son of the goddess began his lament. "I promised Evander that I would protect his son and train him in the ways of war. Now, that gracious king will spend the twilight of his life mourning a dearly loved son. Evander, take comfort in the fact that your son fought bravely. He killed many in his first battle and died while fighting Turnus, the best of our enemies. He comes back to you with great honor."

With that, Aeneas cloaked Pallas in a purple and gold robe, a gift that Dido had sewn. A thousand soldiers, carrying their spears inverted, assembled to escort the body to the Arcadians. Father Aeneas added to the procession horses and armor taken from the enemy. He bound the human sacrifices for the funeral pyre. To show Evander the glory his son had achieved, Aeneas ordered some men to carry tree trunks outfitted with the helmets, corslets, and shields of soldiers Pallas had slain.

After watching the procession disappear into the distance, Aeneas turned to pay his respects at other funeral pyres. But before he could do so, Latin ambassadors bearing olive branches sought a favor: permission to gather their dead and give them a proper burial. Granting the request, Aeneas added, "I only came to Italy because the gods commanded me to do so. We only sought allies and defended ourselves when the Latins and Rutulians attacked us. Justice would be better served if we were to put aside war and Turnus were to face me in hand-to-hand combat."

Drances, a Latin elder, spoke up. "Goddess-born Aeneas, we will carry your words to King Latinus and urge him to reject Turnus and reunite with you."

Under a twelve-day truce, both sides gathered their dead, built funeral pyres, dug graves, and performed the rituals sacred to their people.

Rumor of Pallas' death had already reached the Arcadians. The grieving city met the Trojan procession on the last leg of its journey. Soldiers, their faces wet with tears, lined the road, the torches they held lighting the way. Women, with hair unbound, performed ritual laments, weaving into their songs both shrill cries of grief and criticisms of war. When the procession reached the city walls, no one could hold back King Evander, who flung himself onto his son's body, weeping and moaning. When the sobs had finished wracking his old body, he sang, "What a wretched fate! A father should never survive his son. If only I had been young enough to carry sword and shield against the Rutulians, then these men would have borne me home on this bier instead of you, dear Pallas. But Trojans, I do not blame you, nor do I regret the alliance with the great Aeneas. All I ask, gods, is that you let Aeneas kill Turnus and avenge the death of my son!"

✳✳✳

By the twelfth day of peace, grief had worn out the people of Latium. Few still supported Turnus and his war. Then, word arrived from Diomedes, who, after Achilles, was the best of the Greeks during the Trojan War. He had been King of Argos, but having lost his kingdom, he and his companions came to Italy. The Latin embassy, sent to request his help against the newly arrived Trojans, had now returned with bad news.

"We presented our request," they told Latinus, "but the great hero will not join our battle. He said to us, 'Sons of Italy, the Kingdoms of Saturn, you have inherited the great peace of the Golden Age. Why fight another Trojan War? All of us who recklessly sacked Troy have paid dearly for our sins. We never punished Locrian Ajax for dragging Cassandra from the temple of Minerva. So, on our voyage home, the Battle Goddess scattered the Greek fleet. Her storms drove Menelaus as far as Egypt and Ulysses as far as the Island of the Cyclops. Upon entering his home, Agamemnon was cut down by his wife and her new lover. And because I, in my battle frenzy, wounded the Goddess of Love, she turned my wife adulterous and kept me from my dear homeland. Here in Arpi, the Goddess turned my companions into birds. They haunt our cliffs with their cries, terrified by what has happened to them. So, I urge you, take the beautiful gifts you have brought me and give them to Aeneas. Make a treaty with him. As for my help, I fought the mighty Aeneas once; I have no desire to do so again.'"

For awhile, Latinus sat brooding. He then said, "Diomedes is right. Why are we fighting the son of a goddess? If he is destined to create a homeland here, then we profane the Fates with this war. Here is what I propose: I have land by the Tuscan River that I will give to the Trojans. If this area meets with their approval, they can build their city on it. If not, then we will build them twenty ships so they may search elsewhere in Italy. If this plan meets with the council's approval, I will send a hundred Latins, bearing the olive branch of peace, to form a treaty with Aeneas."

Drances then rose to speak. "King Latinus, your plan is wise and fair. I would only add that you should also marry your daughter to Aeneas. Turnus should put aside his claim and stop wasting Latin lives in his war. If he wants to continue to fight, let him do so. Let him meet Aeneas in hand-to-hand combat."

Turnus had remained quiet throughout the proceedings, still worried that others thought he was a coward for fleeing the battlefield. But now, he was furious. "Drances, you may be an eloquent speaker, but you should leave decisions about the war to the men who actually fight. The Trojans may still hold their fort, but they lost as many as we did in the battle. We have resources. We have allies. So what if Diomedes won't join us? We have Camilla and her Volscians. But if the council decides to withdraw the Latins from this war, then I will fight Aeneas in single combat, even if he carries arms made by Vulcan himself."

Suddenly, a messenger burst through the doors, interrupting the debate. "Aeneas' troops have left their outpost and are marching toward our city!"

People began to panic. Turnus seized the opportunity. "Captains, assemble your troops and get ready to follow me into battle!" The Queen grabbed Lavinia by the wrist, and the two of them joined the city's matrons in offering gifts and prayers at the temple of Minerva. The other civilians rushed to the top of the city's walls.

Camilla, whose passion for war matched Turnus', rode up to the Rutulian leader and said, "With your permission, I will take my Volscians and meet Aeneas' troops in battle while you protect the city."

"Camilla," Turnus replied, "you are the pride of Italy. Here's what I propose. I am preparing troops to ambush Aeneas as he comes through a mountain gorge. While I attend to him, you attack the Etruscan cavalry."

✳✳✳

The Volscians rode onto the field in front of Latinus' city walls. On came the Etruscans, equally powerful riders. When the two sides came within throwing distance, they launched spears and arrows at each other, obscuring the sky the way flocks of starlings do when they seek Roman refuge from frigid northern climes.

Looking down from Olympus, the gods watched as the two sides came crashing into each other. Levelled spears caught opposing riders, whose horses galloped away without them. The Latins turned and rode toward their walls, with Etruscan troops bearing down hard on them. Suddenly, the Latin riders shouted and turned their warhorses to confront the Etruscans, who then turned and fled across the plain. To the gods, the scene looked like the sea surging and ebbing, its waves breaking on the rocky shore and then receding, pulling stones into its foam and leaving the beach dry.

Diana, Goddess of the Hunt, watched her favorite, Camilla, ride into the fray, armor gleaming in the sun, battle-ax slung on her back, spear in her deadly hand. Like an Amazonian queen, the Volscian revelled in the slaughter, taunting the men who fled from her. She unhorsed many riders, and every spear she threw took down an Etruscan warrior. She got the giant Trojan Butes from behind. His companion then chased her, hot for revenge. Suddenly, she spun around and brought down her deadly ax. His brains splattered on her face. A horseman from the Tuscan hills saw the Volscian queen bearing down, quickly mastered his panic, and issued a challenge. "Dismount and face me in hand-to-hand combat." Savoring the opportunity, she did so. The Etruscan soldier, pleased that his trick worked,

sped off on his horse. Fast as Mercur,
chased him down, grabbed the horse's re.
man, like a falcon that catches a dove in it.
until blood and feathers fill the sky.

Now Camilla saw a Trojan in gorgeous arm.
how much honor such a trophy would bring. So
she on her quarry that she didn't realize that the
Arruns was aiming his spear at her. He prayed to
"Protector of Mount Soracte, where we walk barefoot
burning coals, trusting in you to keep us from harm, grant
I kill this warrior who is destroying your Etruscans." Apo.
heard his request and granted it. Arruns launched his spear, anc
it drilled into her side, just beneath her heart. The Volscians
rushed to their queen. She tugged at the spear, but the bronze
head stuck between two of her ribs. Falling from her horse, the
great Camilla bled into the ground. Hateful darkness covered
her eyes.

Fear ruined Arruns' feeling of triumph. He quickly fled, as
a wolf will slink off, its tail between its legs, when it realizes
how rash it was to kill a shepherd.

Diana saw her favorite's death and called upon Opis, one
of her hunting companions. "Take my bow and quiver. You
must avenge Camilla's death." Enraged, Opis bolted from
Olympus. Spotting Arruns, she nocked an arrow, drew back
her bowstring, and loosed death. Arruns fell to the ground, but
none of the soldiers around him noticed. His corpse remained
on the dusty field.

Camilla gone, her troops wheeled around and began to
retreat. The Rutulians and Latins quickly followed, arriving at
the gates only to find them barred. The first group pounded,
and those inside opened the doors just long enough to admit
them quickly. The Etruscans followed the second group so

ly that they all merged at the walls. The men who closed
gates dared not open them a second time, even for their
ading friends. On the walls, mothers, who had gone to fling
wn spears and rocks, saw their sons and husbands
laughtered before their eyes. Some locked-out soldiers spun
their horses around to fight their enemies but ended up
impaling their comrades.

Meanwhile, the Volscian captain Acca sped off to bring
Turnus a message: he must abandon his ambush and defend
the city walls. Enraged, he reluctantly led his troops away from
the mountain pass, which was the will of Jove. Soon after that,
Aeneas and his men crossed the ridge safely. On the plains, the
Trojan army followed so closely that Turnus spun around and
saw Aeneas. The two men would have squared off that day,
but Sol had finished his trip across the day's sky and was
plunging his weary horses in the waters of the Spanish Sea. The
Trojans and their allies pitched their tents and started their
cooking fires while the Latins fortified their walls.

BOOK TWELVE

The Death of Turnus

O nce inside the city gates, Turnus saw fear and despair on everyone's face. All knew that Camilla was dead. Most had participated in the panic-stricken retreat. Now, they saw Aeneas' forces camped just outside their walls.

As he walked toward the palace, Turnus felt the weight of their stares, and his pride bristled at their unspoken accusations. He became even more stubborn in his determination to get rid of the foreigner. Coming before King Latinus, he said, "Tomorrow, I will meet Aeneas in single combat. Either I kill the Trojan and get what you promised me, or he kills me, marries Lavinia, and makes the Italians his slaves. Make the arrangements."

Calmly, the King replied, "I commend your courage, Turnus, but I must proceed carefully. Already, so much trouble has come to the Latins because we defied the gods' will, which Father Faunus had revealed to me. I'm willing to admit defeat, marry my daughter to Aeneas, and have the Trojans as our allies. The Fates decided these matters long ago. There is no reason for you to die. You have your own kingdom and many beautiful, well-born women from which to choose your bride. There's no shame in not fighting the son of the goddess. Instead, you will be honoring the will of the gods and the decision of the Fates."

The King's words only angered Turnus. "You assume that Aeneas will win. I too am a powerful warrior. And if I die, I will still achieve undying fame. Make the arrangements." And with that, Turnus stormed out of the palace.

✳✳✳

Dawn brought her rosy radiance to the world. In his quarters, Turnus dressed for battle. He strapped on his breastplate of gold and bronze and put on a helmet with a blood-red crest. He hefted his shield and took up his father's sword, the one made by Vulcan and dipped in the River Styx. But Aeneas, too, was terrifying when arrayed in the armor he received from his mother.

Each man's army now took its place around the field of battle. They were outfitted for war but planted their spears in the ground and leaned their shields against them. The priests marched to the center, preparing the sacrifices.

Watching these preliminaries from the heights of Olympus, Juno now spoke to Turnus' sister, Juturna. "Nymph of Streams, do not blame me if Turnus falls to Aeneas. I did all I could to protect your brother. Jove has forbidden me to interfere, but you are his sister. It would not be inappropriate for you to do something."

Listening, Juturna continued to cry. Exasperated, Juno said, "Stop. There's no time for tears. Get the war started again. Maybe Turnus can win without fighting Aeneas." Filled with hope, the nymph flowed down from Olympus and into an Italian stream.

✱✱✱

The kings now rode in their chariots to the center of the field. Turnus drove two magnificent white horses. Aeneas' shield, which foretold the future of Rome, shone brightly in the sun. Pouring a libation to the gods, Aeneas declared, "If Turnus defeats me, the Trojans shall withdraw to the city of Evander and my descendants will never renew this war. If I prevail, the Trojans will not subjugate the Italians. Instead, we will be allies and equals. Latinus will keep his throne, and I will name my city Lavinium after his daughter, my wife."

Latinus now poured a libation and stated, "By Jove, whose lightning makes agreements binding, the Italians will never break this treaty, regardless of who wins."

But when the Rutulians saw the two warriors up-close, saw how Aeneas towered over Turnus, they began to feel the fight wasn't fair. Juturna heard their murmurings and took this opportunity to incite them to renew the war. She appeared among them as Camers, one of their most respected warriors, and said, "Just look at how we outnumber their army. We should be ashamed, letting Turnus sacrifice himself. We could easily drive these Trojans from Italy and send their allies running home, beaten. If we let Aeneas kill him in hand-to-hand combat, Turnus will achieve lasting fame, kept alive on the lips of men for generations. But we, we will become slaves; no existence is worse."

Rutulians repeated Juturna's words among themselves. Gradually, their desire for battle spread to Latins and Volscians. Soon, even those who longed for peace were itching to pick up sword and shield. Then the mighty Tolumnius announced, "Today, we save Turnus and take back our pride of place!" With that, he threw his spear across the field. Juturna steered it to the target she had selected, an Etruscan whose eight brothers were standing next to him. The spear punched through his breastplate and ribs, and he fell to the ground, dead. Immediately, his brothers grabbed their weapons and ran to the other side, burning for revenge. A wave of Rutulians raced to meet them. Soon, all the spectators joined the fight. Spears and arrows filled the air. Warhorses crashed, their riders desperate to cut down their enemies. The truce was forgotten.

But steadfast Aeneas, without helmet or shield, reached out to his men and cried, "Stop! What are you doing? We already sealed the treaty with vows and sacrifices. Turnus and I alone have the right to battle." Suddenly, an arrow struck Aeneas in the thigh. As soon as he crumpled to the ground, his men picked him up and led him to his tent.

Seeing his opponent leave the field, Turnus felt a surge of hope and took up his weapons. He leapt into his chariot and whipped his horses into a frenzy. He cut a broad swath through the enemy troops, rolling over the bodies of those who got in his way. Now, letting his charioteer handle the reigns, he dealt out death with spear and sword, taking down many noble Etruscans, Arcadians, and Trojans.

He spotted the mighty Eumedes. His father was Dolon, the swift-runner who had volunteered when Hector needed someone to spy on the Greek camp. But Dolon was captured by Ulysses and Diomedes, who had been stealthily working their way toward the Trojan camp. Ulysses vowed not to kill him if he told them about the new arrivals. When Dolon finished informing them about the Thracians, Diomedes cut off his head and went on to kill Rhesus and steal his great horses.

Spotting Dolon's son, Turnus threw his spear and wounded the man. Then, the Rutulian general stood over him and said, "Take a last look at Italy, whose people you failed to conquer!" He then plunged his sword deep into Eumedes' neck.

Aeneas reached his tent, leaning on his spear and gritting his teeth. He then tried to pull the arrow out of his thigh but found it stuck. Deeply concerned about his father, Ascanius ran to get Iapyx, the army's physician.

When he was a young man, Iapyx caught the attention of Apollo, who promised to give him mastery of the lyre, or prophecy, or archery. But Iapyx declined all of these. Because his father was deathly ill, he asked the god to teach him the art of medicine.

Now, the physician applied healing herbs to Aeneas' wound and attempted to remove the arrowhead. But it would not budge.

Looking down from Olympus, Venus saw her son's pain and raced to Aeneas' tent. Making herself invisible, she crushed a healing herb into water and added ambrosia and panacea. Now when Iapyx used this solution to bathe Aeneas' wound, the son of Venus no longer felt any pain, and the physician easily removed the arrow. Watching the wound close up before his very eyes, Iapyx cried, "Quick! Get this man his weapons. My healing arts did not do this. His mother, the goddess, must want him to return to the battle."

***

Aeneas, surrounded by his mightiest companions, emerged resplendent from his tent. His appearance alone drove the Latins and Rutulians away from the Trojan camp.

While taking on all challengers, Aeneas scanned the battlefield for Turnus. Juturna saw the look on Aeneas' face, like a hungry Persian lion searching for cattle, and quickly devised another strategy to help her brother. She knocked the driver out of Turnus' chariot. She assumed the man's form, took up the reins, and expertly drove through enemy lines. She allowed her brother many kills to increase his glory, but never stayed in one area for very long, for fear that Aeneas would catch up to them.

Aeneas continued to track his prey, racing after the chariot on its winding path and calling out challenges to Turnus. But the Trojan could not ignore those around him. Seeing Messapus, son of Neptune and ally of Turnus, take aim at him, Aeneas dropped to one knee and put up his god-made shield. The spear passed just over its rim and sheared off the crest of Aeneas' helmet. Enraged by the close call, the son of the goddess called upon Jove to witness the violated truce and flew into a killing frenzy.

So, Aeneas and Turnus, widely separated on the field of battle, dealt out death and destruction. Their armies locked in combat, neither side gaining the upper hand for very long.

Venus now put into her son's mind the idea to attack Latinus' city. Aeneas gathered what troops he could and said to them, "All of their soldiers came out to see the battle between Turnus and me. That means Latium is undefended.

We will attack it, and unless they surrender, we will burn it to the ground."

One group stormed the city with ladders and torches. Another group wedged themselves between the walls and the ongoing battle to keep the enemy from coming to Latium's defense. Inside, the citizens panicked. Queen Amata, believing that Turnus was dead and overwhelmed with guilt for causing this war, tore cloth from her garment and wove a noose. Finding her mother dead, Lavinia pulled down her hair, raked her nails down her flawless cheeks, and sent up a loud cry. More and more women joined the lament. Overwhelmed with grief, King Latinus fell to his knees and poured dirt over his head.

✳✳✳

Meanwhile, Turnus' chariot continued its circuitous route at the edges of the battle. But the Rutulian general took less and less joy in his driver's newfound skill. Then, he heard the cries from Latium and, turning, saw the smoke and flames. Grabbing the reins, he ordered his charioteer to take him back to the city. Juturna, still disguised, argued, "We are finding great success here. The Latins can defend their city."

Looking sad, Turnus replied, "Sister, I know it is you. Did you come here to see my disgrace? If it is my time to die, then so be it. I will go down defending the city and avenging my companions. People will not call me a coward. They will remember me as a hero."

Taking up his weapons, Turnus leapt from the chariot. He plowed through the battlefield to get to the city. Arriving, he held up his hand and spoke, "Latins! Rutulians! Stand down. The battle is between Aeneas and me. Glory to the man the Fates have chosen!"

Hearing that voice, Aeneas climbed down from the wall and, exhilarated, clanged his mighty weapons together. The sound was like Jove's thunder.

The two men raced toward each other and launched their spears. Meeting, they fought with sword and shield; the sound of bronze crashing into bronze was deafening. Blocking a blow, Turnus raised his mighty sword and prepared to bring it down on Aeneas' head. Seeing this, the crowd let out a gasp. But suddenly, Aeneas brought up his shield, the one that depicted the future of Rome. Turnus' sword shattered. Looking at the unfamiliar hilt, he realized that, in his haste, he had grabbed his charioteer's sword rather than his own.

Turnus fled, calling on his men to get his sword, the one the immortal blacksmith had dipped in the River Styx. Aeneas gave chase but stopped to retrieve his spear, which was lodged in the trunk of an oak tree. Seeing Aeneas struggling with it, Juturna transformed again into Turnus' charioteer and brought her brother his sword. Venus saw the nymph interfering and decided she would loosen her son's spear.

***

On Olympus, Jove turned to his wife and said, "Juno, I doubt Juturna would have gone against my command unless you put her up to it. No more! I have allowed you to harass the Trojans for long enough."

The Queen of Olympus replied, "I yield. I have grown tired of this war, and it is time for both men to live out their fates. But grant me one request. Let the Latins keep their name and don't make them give up their customs for Trojan ones."

Jove replied, "Since those requests don't contradict the Fates, I will grant them. The Trojans will fade away as they mingle with the Latins. Furthermore, you will find the Romans your greatest worshippers."

Now, Jove sent Juturna an omen. Swooping down from Olympus, a death-owl beat its wings and screeched in Turnus' face. The Rutulian champion shrank back in dread. Juturna recognized the sign, this predictor of death, and cried, "Turnus, my dear brother, I can't prolong your life any longer. Immortality will be miserable without you." She plunged into her stream to grieve.

Aeneas called out, "Turnus, you can't avoid me forever. Stand and fight."

"I'm not afraid of you, foreigner. I fear the will of the gods." With that, Turnus lifted a huge rock, the kind that not even twelve men could lift, such as men are nowadays. But as he went to throw it, a feeling of dread again washed over him. The throw fell short.

Aeneas pulled his spear free of the tree trunk and, with all his might, hurled it at Turnus. It bored through all seven layers of the Rutulian's shield and sliced open his thigh, dropping the mighty warrior to his knees.

Aeneas now stood over Turnus, who lifted his hands to the son of the goddess and said, "You win. Lavinia is yours. I only ask that you pity my aged father and spare him the pain of my death."

Remembering Anchises, Aeneas paused. He had fulfilled his destiny. He would marry the Latin princess and build his homeland on the banks of the Tiber. He was ready to show mercy.

But then he saw that Turnus was wearing Pallas' belt as a trophy. The sight renewed his wrath, and he said, "You didn't show King Evander any mercy when you killed his son. The arm that holds this sword is no longer mine. It is Pallas', and he repays the pain you caused his father."

With that, Aeneas plunged his sword into the Rutulian's chest. Hateful darkness settled over Turnus' eyes, and he breathed out his spirit, which flew groaning to the Underworld.

QUESTIONS FOR DISCUSSION

Book One:

1. What are the two main reasons why Juno harasses Aeneas?

2. Given that Juno knows the Fates have decided that Aeneas will establish the city that will become Rome, why does she try to stop him?

3. Is Aeneas a good leader? Why or why not?

4. When Aeneas tries to bolster the refugees' spirits after the catastrophic storm, he says in Latin, *"forsan et haec olim meminisse iuvabit"* (1.203). Some translators render this as "Perhaps one day it will be a joy to remember even this." Others translate it as "Perhaps one day it will help to remember even this." What is the difference? Which do you think Aeneas is more likely to mean? Why?

5. How does Virgil characterize Jove's point of view?

6. In what ways is Dido similar to Aeneas? In Book One, could she be described as having the virtue of *pietas* (see "A Note to Readers")?

7. Given that Venus knows the Fates have decided that Aeneas will establish the city that will become Rome, why is she so worried about her son that she complains to Jove?

8. Describe Aeneas' reaction to seeing the murals depicting the Trojan War.

Book Two:

1. Does Aeneas see Ulysses as heroic? Why or why not?

2. How is Sinon able to convince the Trojans to believe his story?

3. "And so the lies and tricks of Ulysses did what ten years of war and a thousand ships could not, what godlike Achilles and the great Telamon Ajax failed to do: defeated the might and splendor of Troy." What is the irony that Aeneas implies in the above quotation?

4. What do Troy's sacred objects, their public *penates* symbolize in Book Two?

5. Compare Pyrrhus and Aeneas, especially in terms of *pietas* (see "A Note to Readers").

6. Note the moments when Aeneas falls short of being *pius* (see "A Note to Readers"). How does Venus help him return to the virtue of *pietas*?

7. "And now, Priam, once the mightiest king in Asia, lies on the shore, a headless corpse without a name." Describe the mood (the feeling a writer creates in his or her readers) of this quotation.

8. In what ways is Anchises *pius* (see "A Note to Readers")?

Book Three:

1. What mood (the feeling a writer creates in his or her reader) does Virgil create around the character of Andromache? How does he create this mood?

2. Why might Aeneas be tempted to stay in Buthrotum, Helenus and Andromache's kingdom?

3. Compare Ulysses' interaction with the Cyclops (as the Greek castaway presents it) to Aeneas'. What point is Virgil making?

4. Why does Aeneas seek prophecies from Apollo if he knows he is fated to establish a new homeland in Italy?

Book Four:

1. Compare Dido and Aeneas in Book Four in terms of *pietas* (See "A Note to Readers").

2. How good of a leader is Dido before Cupid makes her fall in love with Aeneas? After?

3. To what extent does Juno want Aeneas and Dido to be married? To what extent does Venus?

4. To what extent does Virgil represent Aeneas and Dido as married?

5. How does Iarbas portray Aeneas in his complaint to Jove? Why does he portray him in these specific ways?

6. To what extent does Aeneas love Dido before Mercury's message? Afterward?

7. Do you think Aeneas is guilty of misleading Dido?

8. Why does Virgil have the reader sympathize with Dido and her relationship with Aeneas only to end Book Four with the inevitability of Aeneas leaving her?

9. Research the Punic Wars and the general Hannibal.

Book Five:

1. To what extent are Juno and Iris responsible for the firing of the Trojan ships?
2. Describe the way in which Virgil characterizes Ascanius in Book Five. How does this contribute to his character's development in the *Aeneid*?

Book Six:

1. Compare the descriptions of the Sibyl before and after Apollo possesses her.
2. Virgil twice references Theseus and Pirithous in Book Six. Compare Aeneas to Virgil's representation of these two heroes.
3. Look at the examples of punishments in Tartarus that the Sibyl gives to Aeneas. How do these stories compare to traits that Virgil gives to Aeneas?
4. What types of behavior earn a person an eternity in Elysium?
5. According to the spirit of Anchises, how does an ideal Roman leader behave? Analyze what he means by each of the three traits he lists.

Book Seven:

1. Like Aeneas, Lavinia has divine ancestors. Who are they? Describe each.
2. Compare Latinus, as he is represented in Book Seven, to Aeneas.
3. What is the name of the envoy who first speaks to King Latinus? With what is that name associated? (Think of what the word "Iliad" refers to.) Why, then, is it significant that these two men first speak of an alliance?

4. What presents do the envoys present to Latinus? What meaning does Virgil imply by these specific gifts being given to Latinus?
5. How does Juno's behavior in Book Seven compare to Venus' behavior in Book Two?
6. Compare how quickly Amata succumbs to Allecto's manipulations to how quickly Turnus succumbs to them. What does the difference imply about Turnus?
7. What is the nature of Amata's complaint when she appeals to the women of Latium?
8. What role does the cult of Bacchus seem to play in the lives of women as compared to men?
9. Research the Gates of Janus.

Book Eight:

1. Research the following allusions: Palatine Hill, the Great Altar of Hercules, guest-friendship, the Morning Star, the first sack of Rome by the Gauls, and Antony and Cleopatra.

Book Nine:

1. Analyze Turnus' reaction to Aeneas' ships turning into nymphs. What does this reveal about his character, especially in comparison to Aeneas'?
2. In Book Nine, what significant developments do we see in Ascanius' character?
3. What characteristics of epic heroes do we find in Nisus and Euryalus? Which of these characteristics does Virgil seem to portray as positive? As negative?
4. How does the inclusion of Euryalus' mother complicate the portrayal of an epic hero?
5. Analyze Virgil's portrayal of war in Book Nine.

Book Ten:

1. Analyze the speeches given by Venus and Juno when the gods meet at the beginning of Book Ten. How do they contribute to Virgil's representation of the Olympians?
2. What are some of the strategic rhetorical moves Venus makes to persuade Jove and the other Olympians that Juno is at fault? Focus on specific details.
3. How does Juno reply to Venus' speech? Is Juno or Venus the better rhetorician?
4. Respect for fathers is an important ideal in the *Aeneid*. Analyze the characters of Turnus and Pallas in relation to this ideal.
5. After Turnus exults in the spoils he took from Pallas' corpse, Jove turns to Hercules and says, "Man cannot see the doom right in front of him. Soon, Turnus will rue the day he exacted such a price from Evander, King of the Arcadians." What literary technique does Virgil use in this quotation?
6. How does Aeneas behave after hearing of Pallas' death?
7. How does Aeneas feel after killing Mezentius' son, Lausus? Why does he feel this way?
8. What is the symbolic importance of the strength of Aeneas' shield?

Book Eleven:

1. How does Virgil represent Aeneas as *pius* in the first three paragraphs of Book Eleven?
2. List the Trojan (and perhaps Roman) customs we see in Book Eleven. What qualities or ideals do the funeral customs seem to honor?

3. Describe the attitude Aeneas, the Latins, and Diomedes each have about war in Book Eleven.
4. Research the relationship between Saturn, the Golden Age, and Italy.
5. How do Diomedes' speech and Latinus' response to it stress the importance of respecting the gods?
6. Characterize Camilla.

Book Twelve:

1. Why might it be important that the sword Turnus takes into battle is made by Vulcan and dipped in the River Styx?
2. How does Aeneas' vow to Latinus before the dual with Turnus reflect the Roman ideals preached by Anchises in Book Six?
3. Re-read the story of Dolon in Book Twelve. Both Ulysses and Diomedes appear elsewhere in the *Aeneid*. Compare how they were represented earlier to how they are represented here.
4. What theme is exemplified in the story of how the physician Iapyx learned his art from Apollo?
5. Describe how Aeneas' response to the renewal of war contributes to his characterization.
6. Describe how Turnus changes throughout Book Twelve.
7. Why does Virgil include the specifics that he does in the negotiation between Jove and Juno?
8. Describe Aeneas' thoughts and emotions as he prepares to kill Turnus at the end of Book Twelve. In what ways is the ending consistent with the characterization of Aeneas in the Aeneid? In what ways is it inconsistent?

9. Why do you think Virgil ends the *Aeneid* in the way that he does?

GLOSSARY AND
PRONUNCIATION OF NAMES

After each name, its pronunciation (divided into syllables, the stressed syllable in capital letters) follows.

Acestes (ah-KES-teez): a Trojan hero who played host to Aeneas' people and who became the founding king of Acesta in Sicily.

Achates (ah-KA-teez): Aeneas' companion-in-arms.

Achilles (ah-KIL-eez): son of the sea goddess Thetis and the mortal Peleus; the mightiest of the Greek heroes in the Trojan War. When Agamemnon needed to return his female captive to her father in order to appease Apollo, he takes Achilles' slave Briseis. Seeing this as an incredible insult, Achilles refuses to fight for the Greeks and remains in his tent with the troops he brought with him. Achilles rejoins the fight when his companion-in-arms Patroclus is killed by Hector. Achilles then kills Hector.

Aegis (EE-jis): owned by Jove but often in Minerva's possession, its exact nature is unclear, but it is always said to be awful to behold, with a gorgon's head in its center; sometimes it is represented as a shield, that Jove will shake to cause thunder or that Minerva will shake to rout opposing troops in a battle; sometimes it is represented as a breastplate of burnished gold with a surface like snakeskin; originally, it seems to have been a goatskin covering worn over the shoulder of the non-shield-bearing hand.

Aeneas (uh-NEE-us or ee-NEE-us or eye-NAY-ahs): son of the goddess Venus and the mortal Anchises; second mightiest of the Trojan heroes in the Trojan War; leader of the Trojan refugees after the fall of Troy. Titles like "Father," "Pious," and "Steadfast" are often attached to his name.

Agamemnon (a-ga-MEM-non): King of Mycenae; the most powerful of the Greek kings and thus the head of their army in the Trojan War; brother of Menelaus; sacrificed his virgin daughter Iphigenia to appease Diana, who would not let the Greeks sail to Troy until he had done so.

Alba Longa (AL-ba LON-ga): a city in west-central Italy founded by Ascanius.

Allecto (ah-LEC-toe): one of the three Furies; Juno commands her to bring about a war between the Latins and Aeneas' Trojans.

Anchises (an-KEYE-seez): a member of the royal family of Troy; father of Aeneas by Venus; escapes the fall of Troy on his son's shoulders.

Amata (ah-MA-ta): King Latinus' wife; Queen of the Latins; strongly supports her daughter Lavinia's marriage to Turnus.

Andromache (an-DRA-ma-kee): wife of Hector; mother of Astyanax; Pyrrhus' captive after the Fall of Troy; wife of Helenus after she is abandoned by Pyrrhus.

Anna (AN-a): sister of Dido.

Antony (AN-toh-nee): a Roman politician and general, who was a supporter of Julius Caesar and who later was one of the three dictators that made up the Second Triumvirate. He became a great rival of Octavian (later, given the title Augustus Caesar.) While ruling over Rome's eastern provinces, Antony carried on a love affair with Egypt's Cleopatra. Hostilities between Octavian and Antony erupted into civil war, and Antony was defeated by Octavian's forces at the Battle of Actium.

Apollo (ah-POL-oh): god of music, light, prophecy, archery, healing, and purification; twin brother of Diana; son of Jove and the Titan Latona ("Leto" in Greek).

Arcadia (ar-KAY-dee-uh): region in Greece; original home of Evander and those who founded Pallanteum in Italy.

Ascanius (as-KAY-nee-us): also called Iulus; son of Aeneas and Creusa; escapes from the fall of Troy with his father; later, founder of Alba Longa.

Astyanax (as-TEYE-an-ax); son of Hector and Andromache; killed during the Fall of Troy.

Atlas (AT-las): Titan who holds up the sky.

Augustus Caesar (aw-GUHS-tuhs or uh-GUHS-tuhs SEE-zer): First known as Octavian, he was adopted by Julius Caesar and named as his heir. A political and military leader. Along with Marc Antony and Marcus Lepidus, he was one of the three dictators that made up the Second Triumvirate. Hostilities between Octavian and Antony erupted into civil war, and Octavian's forces defeated Antony at the Battle of Actium. He was the first emperor of Rome, reigning from 27 BCE to his death in 14 CE

Bacchus (BAK-us): son of Jove and the mortal Semele; god of wine and ecstatic celebration; his followers were wild women known as Maenads or Bacchae or Bacchantes.

Camilla (ca-MILL-ah): similar to the Amazonian Penthesilea in Greek mythology, Camilla is a female warrior, dear to Diana. She leads her Volscians into battle against Aeneas' forces.

Carthage (KAR-thaj): city on the shore of Libya in northwest Africa, founded by Dido and her Phoenician followers, who were escaping from Tyre; historically, a rival of Rome; an enemy of Rome in the Punic Wars.

Cassandra (kuh-SAN-druh): daughter of Priam and Hecuba; sister of Hector, Paris, Helenus, etc., a seer cursed by Apollo so her prophecies would never be believed; during the Fall of Troy, the Greek Ajax the Lesser (or Oileus Ajax) dragged her from her place of sanctuary in Minerva's temple and raped her.

Centaur (SEN-tor): a creature with the head, torso, and arms of a man and the body, legs, and tail of a horse.

Charon (CARE-uhn): ferryman of spirits across the River Styx in the Underworld.

Charybdis (ka-RIB-dis): a mythical whirlpool in the straits of Messina (between Sicily and Italy), across from the cave of the monster Scylla.

Chimaera (kigh-MEE-rah): a fire-breathing monster with a lion's head, a goat's body, and a serpent's tail; killed by the hero Bellerophon.

Cupid (KYOO-pid): son of Venus; minion of Venus; often depicted as a young man or young boy with wings and armed with a bow and arrows; his arrows kindle desire in those he wounds with them.

Cybele (SIB-eh-lee or KEE-bel-ee): see "Great Mother of the Gods."

Cyclops (SEYE-klops) singular; Cyclopes (SEYE-klo-peez) plural: a gigantic creature with one eye in the middle of his or her forehead; lives on the island of Sicily.

Daedalus (DED-l-uhs or DEED-l-uhs): an Athenian master craftsman who built the Labyrinth, a huge maze located under the palace of King Minos in Crete, to contain the Minotaur. Minos imprisoned Daedalus and his son in a tower in order to protect the solution to the Labyrinth. Daedalus built wings for himself and his son, Icarus, so they could escape. Icarus forgot his father's advice, flew too close to the sun, which melted the wax holding the feathers to the wings, and plummeted to his death. Daedalus himself landed on the island of Sicily where he built a temple to the god Apollo.

Dardanus (DAHR-dan-us): founder of Troy, who according to Virgil, came from Italy; the Trojans are sometimes called Dardanians after him.

Delos (DEE-los): a very small island in the Aegean Sea where Apollo was born and where he had one of his two most famous oracles.

Deiphobus (dee-IF-uh-bus): son of Priam and Hecuba; brother of Hector, Paris, Helenus, and Cassandra; husband of Helen after Paris was killed; one of this mightiest Trojan Warriors during the Trojan War.

Diana (dye-AN-ah): virgin goddess of the hunt; twin sister of Apollo; daughter of Jove and the Titan Latona ("Leto" in Greek).

Dido (DEYE-doh or DEE-doh): also known as Elissa; founding queen of Carthage after she fled her husband Sychaeus' murder by her brother, King Pygmalion of Tyre.

Diomedes (die-oh-MEE-deez): son of Tydeus, who was one of the Seven Against Thebes; King of Argos; one of the mightiest Greek heroes during the Trojan War; often Ulysses' partner on his exploits, including the slaughter of Rhesus and the stealing of the Palladium; famously fought Aeneas to the latter's near-death and wounded Venus; founded Argyripa (later Arpi) in Italy after the Trojan War; one of Minerva's favorite heros, some accounts say she made him immortal upon his death.

Dolon (DOH-lon): a Trojan soldier; volunteers when Hector calls for someone to spy on the Greek camps in Book X of the *Iliad*; caught by Ulysses and Diomedes, he bargains for his life by telling them about the arrival of Rhesus and the Thracian army, only to be killed by Diomedes; his son Eumedes is killed by Turnus in the final day of the war.

Drances (DRAN-seez): a Latin elder who argues against following Turnus.

Elysium (ih-LEE-zhee-uhm): the place in the Underworld where the spirits of the blessed dwell.

Etruscans (ee-TRUS-cans): the people of Etruria, a region north of Rome, who join Aeneas' army and fight against the Latins and Rutulians.

Euryalus (you-REE-a-lus): a young Trojan soldier and dear companion of the older Nisus.

Evander (ee-VAN-der): King of the Arcadians at Pallanteum in Italy; father of the hero Pallas, who fights for Aeneas in the war against the Latins.

Fates: also called *Parcae*; three goddesses who spin the threads of destiny.

Faunus (FAW-nus): a horned god of the forest and countryside, who came to be equated with the Greek god Pan; one of the oldest Roman deities; according to Virgil, he was also a legendary king of the Latins and the father of Latinus.

Gates of Janus: the double doors of an untraditional temple in the Roman Forum that was dedicated to Janus, the two-faced god of boundaries; its double doors, called "the gates of war," were open during times of war and closed during times of peace.

Gauls (GAWLZ): a group of Celtic people of Western Europe during the Iron Age and the Roman period; they were often at war with the Romans; a group of Gauls in northern Italy sacked Rome in 390 BCE, during which (according to legend) they tried to invade Capitoline Hill during the night, but a flock of geese sacred to Juno alerted the Roman guards, who killed them.

Glaucus (GLAW-kuss): a captain in the Lycian army (allied with Troy) under the command of his cousin Sarpedon during the Trojan War; helped defend the body of his dying commander; killed by Telamon Ajax during the fight for the corpse of Achilles.

Gorgons (GORE-gon): three sisters who have snakes for hair and visages so terrifying that those who look upon them are turned to stone; two of the sisters were immortal, but the third (Medusa) was not and was beheaded by the hero Perseus.

Great Mother of the Gods, the: also known as Cybele (SIB-eh-lee or KEE-bel-ee); her full official Roman name was Mater Deum Magna Idaea (Great Idaean Mother of the Gods), thus her association with Mount Ida in the *Aeneid.* The Romans identified her with Ops and other goddesses. Most importantly, she symbolizes universal motherhood, having given life not only to the gods, but also to human beings and beasts.

Harpies (HAR-peez): creatures with the bodies of birds and the heads of women, known for snatching food or fouling it with their excrement, which they most famously do to King Phineus in the story of Jason and the Argonauts.

Hecate (hek-UH-tee): underworld goddess of magic and witchcraft, associated with night, the moon, and the crossroads; sometimes portrayed as triple-bodied.

Hector (HEK-tor): oldest son of King Priam and Queen Hecuba; the mightiest of the Trojan heroes during the Trojan War; husband of Andromache and father of Astyanax; killed Patroclus; killed by Achilles, who dragged Hector's corpse from the back of a chariot he drove around the walls of Troy.

Hecuba (hek-YOU-ba): Queen of Troy; wife of King Priam; mother of Hector, Paris, Helenus, Cassandra, and others; taken as a captive by the Greeks during the fall of Troy.

Helen (HEH-len): daughter of Jove and the mortal Leda; step-daughter of King Tyndareus; the most beautiful woman in the world; Venus offers her as a bribe to Paris in order to win the contest for the Golden Apple; wife of King Menelaus, who waged the Trojan War to get her back after she went with or was taken by Paris to Troy.

Helenus (HEH-len-us): son of Priam and Hecuba; brother of Hector, Paris, Cassandra, etc.; seer whose prophecies, unlike Cassandra's, were believed; captured by Pyrrhus during the Sack of Troy; became the king of Epirus and husband of Andromache after Pyrrhus' death.

Hesperia (hes-PER-ee-ah): another name for Italy.

Hydra (HI-dra): a gigantic, nine-headed water-serpent, which haunted the swamps of Lerna; destroyed by Hercules as one of his twelve labors.

Iarbas (YAR-bas): son of Jupiter Ammon and a Libyan nymph; North African king; sold Dido a piece of land, on which she founded Carthage; seeks Dido's hand in marriage and calls upon his father when he hears she has married Aeneas.

Icarus (IK-er-uhs): see Daedalus.

Ilia (IL-ee-ah): priestess of Vesta; mother of Romulus and Remus by Mars.

Iulus (ee-OO-lus): another name for Ascanius, son of Aeneas and Creusa.

Iris (EYE-ris): one of the Olympian messenger gods; goddess of the rainbow; Greek ceramic art portrays her as a young woman with wings.

Janus: Roman god of beginnings, transitions, and entrances. See also "Gates of Janus."

Jove (JOHV): also called Jupiter; king of the gods; god of thunder, lightning, and the sky; husband of Juno; father (with various mothers) of the Olympians Apollo, Diana, Mars, Venus (sometimes), Bacchus, Mercury, and Minerva.

Julius Caesar (JOOL-yuhs SEE-zer): 100 BCE to 44 BCE; Roman dictator, politician, and military general, who played a central role in the events leading to the demise of the Roman Republic and the rise of the Roman Empire; Virgil makes him a descendant of Aeneas through Ascanius Iulus; Octavian, later known as Augustus Caesar, was his adopted heir.

Juturna (joo-TURN-ah): water nymph and goddess of springs, wells, and fountains; she supports her brother Turnus against Aeneas and retreats to her waters when she cannot save him.

Laocoon (lay-AK-oh-on): Trojan priest of Neptune; warns the Trojans about the wooden horse; he and two sons are killed by twin sea serpents, which convinces the Trojans to bring the wooden horse inside the walls of Troy.

Latium (LAY-she-um): region of central western Italy ruled by King Latinus.

Lausus (LAU-sus): an ally of Turnus; son of the ousted Etruscan king Mezentius; falls to Aeneas while protecting his injured father.

Lavinia: (luh-VIN-ee-uh): daughter of Turnus and Amata; after the events of the Aeneid, she is married to Aeneas, who names his city (Lavinium) after her.

Lethe (LEE-thee): river in the Underworld; by drinking from its waters, the dead forget their past lives.

Leda (LEE-da): impregnated by Jove while he is in the form of a swan; mother of Helen; wife of King Tyndareus.

Libya (LIB-ee-ah): coastal region of North Africa.

Mars (MARZ): son of Jove and Juno; god of war; father of Romulus and Remus.

Menelaus (meh-neh-LAY-us): husband of Helen; brother of Agamemnon; King of Sparta; Greek hero in the Trojan War; driven by storms to Egypt after the Trojan War.

Mercury (mer-CURE-ee): son of Jove and the nymph Maia (a daughter of Atlas); one of the Olympian messenger gods; often depicted as wearing winged sandals and carrying the Caduceus; conducts the three goddesses to Paris; conducts spirits to Erebus.

Messapus (mes-APP-us): son of Neptune; King of Etruria; ally of Turnus; neither fire nor steel can kill him; Euryalus steals his helmet during a nighttime raid in Book 9.

Mezentius (mez-EN-tee-us): a tyrant who ruled over the Etruscans until they revolted; he escaped to the Rutulians and was protected by Turnus; his son, Lausus, is killed by Aeneas; he too is killed by Aeneas.

Minerva (min-ER-va): born a fully armed adult female from the head of Jove; goddess of battle wisdom; keeper of the aegis; strongly supported the Greeks in the Trojan War; closely supports many Greek heroes including Perseus, Diomedes, and Odysseus/Ulysses.

Maenads (MAY-nads): female followers of Bacchus, who were put into a state of ecstatic frenzy by wine and dancing; they were often portrayed running through forests or mountains, screaming, ripping to pieces and eating any animal they came across.

Neoptolemus (nee-op-TAL-eh-mus): another name for Pyrrhus.

Neptune (NEP-tune): brother of Jove; god of the sea, the earthquake, and the horse.

Nisus (NEYE-sus): Trojan soldier and companion of the younger Euryalus.

Ocean: the river that circled the flat Earth.

Olympus (o-LIM-pus): the mountain on top of which lived the Olympian Gods.

Orestes (o-RES-teez): son of Agamemnon and Clytemnestra; famous for avenging his father's murder; kills Pyrrhus for taking Hermione, to whom Orestes was engaged to be married.

Paris: son of King Priam and Queen Hecuba of Troy; judged the contest for the Golden Apple; accepted Venus' bribe of Helen; his affair with Helen caused the Trojan War; with Apollo's help, kills Achilles; killed shortly before the Fall of Troy.

Palamedes (pal-AH-medz): King of Euboea; framed for treason by Ulysses and executed. The Homeric epics don't mention Palamedes. In Sinon's story in Book 2, Virgil does not give a reason why Ulysses hated Palamedes. According to the *Fabulae* attributed to Hyginus (64 BC-17 AD), Agamemnon himself chose Palamedes for an important diplomatic mission. When the beautiful Helen went with Paris, Menelaus called upon the Greeks who had sworn to protect Helen's marriage to go with him to Troy. Ulysses now had a young bride and a newborn son, so he didn't obey the first summons. Palamedes was sent to Ithaca to persuade the man. He found cunning Ulysses, pretending to be insane, behind a plow yoked to an ox and an ass and sowing salt into his field. Palamedes was not fooled and took Ulysses' infant son and laid it in the path of the plow. Ulysses swerved to avoid the child, thus showing he wasn't insane. He was then honor-bound to answer Menelaus' summons.

Palladium (puh-LAY-dee-uhm): a wooden statue of Pallas Athena (Minerva) that protected Troy; stolen by Ulysses and Diomedes towards the end of the Trojan War.

Pallas (PAL-ass): (1) another name for Minerva; (2) an ancestor of Evander; (3) son of Evander, who fights for Aeneas in the war with the Latins; killed by Turnus.

Patroclus (puh-TROH-kluhs): Achilles' closest companion-in-arms; in the *Iliad*, he persuades Achilles to let him wear his armor and lead their troops, so that the Trojans will think he is Achilles and retreat from the Greek ships, which they are burning; at this time, Patroclus is killed by Hector, which causes an enraged Achilles to re-enter the war in order to kill Hector.

Penates (puh-NAH-teez): in Roman religion, worshipped privately as protectors of the household and publically as protectors of the Roman state.

Pirithous (pie-RITH-ew-uhs): Greek hero; King of the Lapiths. At his wedding to Hippodamia, the Battle of the Lapiths and the Centaurs (also known as the Centauromachy) broke out. Later, he helped his companion, the Athenian hero Theseus, abduct the young Helen (to be Theseus' future wife), and then they attempted to abduct Proserpina, wife of Pluto and Queen of the Underworld (to be Pirithous' wife). When Pluto suspected what they were up to, he invited them to sit and they found themselves bound to the Chairs of Forgetfulness. In some versions, Pluto allows Hercules to rescue Theseus but not Pirithous. In the *Aeneid*, they both remain bound.

Polites (poh-LIE-teez): son of Priam and Hecuba; killed by Pyrrhus in front of Priam.

Polydorus (poh-lee-DOOR-us): son of Priam and Hecuba; sent to the King of Thrace for safekeeping during the Trojan War; when Troy fell, the King killed him; Aeneas hears his spirit and finds his body when the Trojan refugees visit Thrace.

Pluto (ploo-TOW): God of the Underworld; brother of Jove; husband of Proserpina.

Polyphemus (poly-FEE-mus): a Cyclops living on Sicily; blinded by Ulysses.

Priam (PRY-am): King of Troy during the time of the Trojan War; husband of Hecuba; father of Hector, Paris, Cassandra, Helenus, and others; Pyrrhus slays him at an altar during the fall of Troy.

Proserpina (pro-SUR-puh-nuh): the Roman name for Persephone; daughter of Jove and Ceres; wife of Pluto; Queen of the Dead.

Pygmalion (pig-MALE-ee-on): King of Tyre; brother of Dido; slays her husband, Sychaeus.

Pyrrhus (PEER-us): also known as Neoptolemus; son of Achilles, who comes to Troy after his father's death in the last year of the war; takes Andromache as a captive during the fall of Troy; leaves her to marry Hermione; killed by Agamemnon's son, Orestes.

Rhesus (REE-sus): King of Thrace during the Trojan War, he brought his army to fight for Priam; before he could engage in battle, he was killed in his sleep by Ulysses and Diomedes, who were on a night raid and stole his magnificent white horses; his story is told in Book X of the *Iliad*.

Romulus (RAHM-you-lus): son of Mars and the mortal Ilia; brother of Remus; descendent of Aeneas; legendary founder of Rome.

Rutulians (roo-TUL-ee-anz): tribe in Italy; led by Turnus.

Saturn (SAT-urn): a Roman agricultural deity; equivalent to the Greek Cronus; father of Jove, Juno, Neptune, Pluto, Ceres; driven from Olympus by Jove, he then ruled Italy during the peaceful and prosperous Golden Age.

Sarpedon (sahr-PEE-don): Lycian prince; commander of the Lycian army, which was allied with Troy during the Trojan War; son of Zeus; killed by Patroclus.

Scamander (ska-MAN-der): a river near Troy.

Scylla (SIL-a): a monster that snatched and ate men from ships passing through the straits of Messina (between Sicily and Italy); her cave is across from the whirlpool Charybdis.

Sibyl (SIB-ill): prophetess at Cumae in Italy; Aeneas' guide to the Underworld.

Simois (SIM-oh-is): a river near Troy.

Sinon (SIGH-non): a Greek who posed as someone who escaped being a human sacrifice in order to persuade the Trojans to bring the wooden horse inside the walls of Troy.

Sol (SOLE): the Roman sun god, equivalent to the Greek Helios; grandfather of Latinus.

Styx (STIKS): river in the Underworld, across which only the buried may cross.

Sychaeus (see-KEYE-us): husband of Dido before she founded Carthage; murdered by Pygmalion.

Theseus (THEE-see-uhs or THEE-syoos): Greek hero; King of Athens. He is best known for killing the Minotaur. He escaped from Crete with the Cretan Princess Ariadne, who had helped him solve the Labyrinth. He abandoned her on the island of Naxos, either of his own free will or because Bacchus wanted to marry her. Theseus and his companion Pirithous, King of the Lapiths, abducted the young Helen (to be Theseus' future wife) and attempted to abduct Proserpina, wife of Pluto and Queen of the Underworld (to be Pirithous' wife). When Pluto suspected what they were up to, he invited them to sit and then found themselves bound to the chairs of forgetfulness. In some versions, Pluto allows Hercules to rescue Theseus but not Pirithous. In the *Aeneid*, they both remain bound.

Thrace (THREYS): area north-east of Ancient Greece.

Tiber (TIE-bur): river in Italy that flows through the city of Rome; it starts in the Apennine Mountains and empties into the Tyrrhenian Sea (part of the Mediterranean Sea). A popular name for the Tiber was *Flavus* ("the blond"), for its yellowish water.

Tithonus (tith-OH-nus): mortal lover of Dawn/Aurora; given immortality but not eternal youth.

Turnus (TURN-us): king of the Rutulians; the favored suitor of Lavinia, King Latinus' daughter, until the arrival of Aeneas; led the Italian armies against Aeneas' army.

Ulysses (YOO-lis-eez): Roman name for Odysseus, the Greek hero of the Trojan War; a strong warrior, he is more often associated with tricks, lies, and clever ruses, such as the wooden horse.

Venus (VEE-nus): goddess of passion; daughter of Jove; mother of Cupid; mother of Aeneas by the mortal Anchises; wins the contest for the Golden Apple after bribing Paris with Helen; allied with Troy in the Trojan War.

Vesta (VES-ta or WES-ta): virgin goddess of the hearth.

Volscians (VUHL-shun): Italian tribe; allied with Turnus; led by Camilla.

Vulcan (VUHL-kuhn): Roman god of fire and blacksmithing; husband of Venus; makes the armor of Aeneas.

ABOUT THE AUTHOR

Frank Hering earned his B.A. in English from the University of Chicago and his M.A. and Ph.D. in English from the University of Florida. He has taught 9th- and 11th-grade English classes at Elgin Academy in Illinois since 2004. He frequently teaches the *Odyssey* and parts of the *Iliad* and the *Aeneid* to his Freshmen.

What Did You Think of
Virgil's Aeneid Retold for Young Adults?

Thank you for purchasing this book. I hope you enjoyed it and found it useful. I would appreciate it if you would post an honest review on Amazon and share it to Facebook and Twitter. Please feel free to send any questions, comments, or suggestions to me via email (frankhering@att.net).